Battle at Gun Barrel Canyon

There is only one law in Gun Barrel Valley out in the wilds of Montana: the law of the gun.

Old frontiersman, Joshua Vincent, is incensed that his fence wire is being cut and his stock rustled. Chief suspect is his northern neighbour, the young rancher, Matthew Saunders. So, he sends assassins to kill him and range war threatens to erupt.

Meanwhile, pretty Polly Vincent is being held prisoner at her uncle's ranch, subjected to the lascivious attentions of her cousin, Grat, who vows to make her his wife.

As bullets fly Matthew buckles on his trusty Peacemaker. Can he rescue Polly? Can Matthew fight back against Vincent's overwhelming firepower?

Battle at Gun Barrel Canyon

Wolf Lundgren

A Black Horse Western

ROBERT HALE · LONDON

Typeset by
Derek Doyle & Associates, Shaw Heath
Printed and bound in Great Britain by
CPI Antony Rowe, Chippenham and Eastbourne

ONE

Three riders came out of the dark spruces that clothed the steep mountainside, a forbidding air about them with their high-crowned Stetsons, their torn macinaws, and the carbines stuck in their saddle boots as they hauled in their sweating mustangs and peered down at Washoe City.

'Some city,' their leader scoffed, for this town, half-lost in the wilds of Montana, was just a ram-shackle collection of pitch-roofed cabins scattered along a muddy canyon.

'Shouldn't pose no problems, Mace,' an older man, Abe, muttered, as he jerked a long-barrelled Remington revolver from his holster, spun the cylinder and inserted a couple of .44s from his gunbelt with grim assertiveness.

'We'll go do what we come to do then go get our due.' The leader raked vicious spurs along the blood-crusted ribs of his long-suffering mount. 'Hagh!'

Blue smoke drifted from chimneys beneath the dark, snow-threatening sky as they careered their horses down through the rocks and shale of the slope. When they reached the rutted trail that wound down through the town they slowed to a more cautious pace.

'What a hell-hole,' the younger rider, Seth, sneered as they manoeuvred through the potholes, discarded logs and rubbish piles that adorned the so-called main street. 'Glad we ain't gotta stay here long.'

All appeared peaceful on this Monday morning as well-wrapped women with buckets and brooms attended to their chores, their snotty brats splashed each other in puddles, and storekeepers on the sidewalks paused to watch the strangers go clipping by.

Washoe City encompassed all the squalor of a newly-settled Montana town, its timber-framed buildings of cottonwood boards already warped by the region's fierce weather.

'That tinpot bank wouldn't take much bustin',' Seth giggled, as they cantered past.

'We ain't here for that,' Mason growled, jerking his eye-bulging mustang to a halt outside Washoe Saloon, its façade crudely painted in red with the words, 'Music' – 'Darnsin' – 'Eats' – 'Drinks' – 'Gals'.

'Maybe we kin make the bank our next assignment 'fore we mosey on,' Abe rejoined.

The crop-haired saloon keeper, Gus Brown,

paused from watering down whiskey as the three *hombres* clattered into the bar. Almost as big and hairy as a bear, he put aside his funnel and bottle, wiped his hands on his apron and greeted them. 'Marnin', gents. What's ya poison?'

The leader, Mason, propped his Winchester carbine against the bar, peeled off his worn gloves, his eyes cold as ice beneath the wide brim of a once-white, now sweat-stained Stetson. He turned to case the saloon. Customers at this hour were sparse.

'Whiskey.'

'Certainly, sir. Nuthin' like a belly-warmer.' The burly Brown plonked three half-pint tumblers before them and filled them to the brim. 'That's one dollar. This is a pay-as-you-drink bar. I cain't afford no bad debts.'

Mason picked up his tumbler. 'Put it on the slate.'

'What slate? You don't have a slate.'

Young Seth giggled. 'Put it on the slate we don't have, dimbrain.' He waggled his Smith & Wesson self-cocker under the barkeep's nose, then spun it on his finger.

Mason took a slug of the whiskey, grimaced and spat it into the barkeep's surprised face. 'Wadda ya call this?' He tossed the rest of the glass over him. 'Give us a bottle of the best, you cheatin' freak.'

A youth, sprawled on a sagging horsehair sofa, gave a coyote-like cackle. 'Good on you, mister. I been wanting to do that fer years.'

'Who the hell asked you, short-arse?' Mason gave him a spine-chilling glare.

The boy, red-haired and wiry, was jiggling in one hand some silver dollars, and in the other the breasts of a painted whore perched on his knee. The grin was suddenly wiped from his face.

Mason glared at five men huddled around the greasy green baize of a poker table at the saloon's far end, who quickly looked away and returned to their game.

The barkeep was stumbling around, wiping stinging liqour from his eyes and trying to find a bottle of the best brandy among the cobwebs under the bar.

'Hurry it up, bonehead,' Mason snarled, as Gus emerged victorious, brandishing the three star bottle. 'That looks more like the real McCoy.'

'I bin savin' it fer a special occasion.' Gus pulled out the cork with his teeth and spat it out. 'Even I cain't afford this, gents. Special import three dollars a bottle.'

'Put it on the bill.' Mason took a cheroot from a jar on the bar and snapped it between his thin, rat-trap lips. 'I'm looking for a man called Saunders. I'm informed he rides into this town every Monday morning. Where is he?'

The youth on the sofa suddenly dropped his doxie unceremoniously on to the floorboards and Gus looked exasperated.

'Saunders? No, sir, I got no idea,' Gus said.

'Come off it. He runs the Longbranch Ranch to the north of this here Gun Barrel Valley. Where is he?'

The wild-eyed youth on the sofa had got to his feet, swinging to one side the Sidewinder six-gun slung from his hip and taking a stance. 'My name's Jeb Riley. Whadda ya want? Matt's my brother.'

'That's better.' Mason took a bite of his brandy, sampling it. He eyed the poker players malevolently. They shook their heads and quickly returned to their cards, counting themselves out of this. 'Nice drink. Got fire an' guts in its belly. Not like you scum.'

'Yassuh.' Gus eyed the sawn-off beneath his bar but decided it was out of the question. Humour these guys. That's what he had to do. He gave a lecherous wink. 'I got a nice coupla cuties in the back room. Only a dollar an hour to you.'

Mason returned his gaze to Jeb. 'You must be the drunken, whoring young half-brother. You ain't no good to me. I'm looking for Matthew Saunders. I ain't gonna say it again.'

'He ain't in town today.' Jeb's face was reddening to match the colour of his hair at the insults and he struggled to hold his temper. 'We didn't need much so he sent me instead. I'm gonna get us a few supplies.'

'What,' Seth jeered. 'Like wire cutters?'

'Yeah,' Abe put in. 'Some bastards cut a mile-length of wire separating Mr Joshua Vincent's land

9

from yourn. Mr Vincent don't like trespassers, your cows encroaching on his grass. He ain't at all pleased.'

'Shut your mouth, Abe,' Mason spat out. 'I'll do the talking.'

'There's many a man round here hates barbed wire,' Jeb shouted. 'They believe in the freedom of the open range like it allus has been. Why should Vincent blame us?'

'Listen, boy.' Mason trickled smoke from the cheroot through his thin lips. 'I ain't int'rested in what the organ-grinder's monkey got to say. Where is he?'

A bushy-bearded, bald-headed old-timer was sat on a wooden chair in front of a log fire, staring at the blaze and sipping from a tumbler of watered whiskey, apparently oblivious to the proceedings.

Seth wandered over to him. 'Maybe this smelly bag of bones can enlighten us.' He tipped his own brandy over Harold Hawkins's head. 'Hey! *Matt Saunders*,' he shouted. 'Where is he, grandad?'

Hawkins leapt like a startled rat, his eyes bulging, licking his tongue out at the liqour trickling down his face, grinning toothless gums at Seth, making gurgling baby sounds. Waving a hand at him like some lunatic.

'Ain't no use askin' Harold,' the barkeep muttered. 'He's a deaf mute. Bats in the attic.'

'Oh, yeah,' Seth jeered. 'Give us a hand, Abe.

We'll soon make him squeal.'

He piled more logs on the fire as the older man joined him and they grabbed Harold by his arms, spreading him back across the brick firebreast as flames roared up the chimney. 'Howja like a hot arse, oldtimer?'

Harold wriggled and spluttered out looney groans as the seat of his overalls began to sizzle, the legs smouldering, but he was held tight, his eyes bulging even wider. For five long minutes he withstood the torture.

'Look at them lice leapin' outa his underpants fer safety,' Abe cackled, and even the poker players now watching had to guffaw. 'Bet there ain't much entertainment like this in Washoe City, eh, fellas?'

'Yep, better'n the music hall,' Seth hollered. 'Ain't it?'

'He's over at the bank!' Harold screamed, still wriggling and kicking like a hooked fish.

'Good golly! Praise the Lord,' Seth intoned. 'It's a miracle. The ol' fool's regained his speech.'

'Yeah.' Abe picked up Harold's whiskey and tossed it on the fire. Flames belched out. 'How's he like that?'

His captors stood back, laughing, as Hawkins leapt for safety in a cloud of smoke from his singed backside. 'Looks even more like a dirty burned spud now, don't he?'

'Over at the bank, is he?' Mason mused. 'Right,

we'll just wait here nice'n quiet shall we? You milk-sops at the far end unbuckle ya gunbelts and drop 'em in the corner. Move!'

While the poker players obeyed his order, Mason turned his Winchester on Jeb. 'You, half-pint, take that shooter from your belt nice an' slowly. No tricks. Or do ya fancy tryin' me?'

Jeb bristled at the insult to his five foot three stature but did as he was bid using thumb and fore-finger to slide his slim, twelve-inch long Sidewinder from his belt by its staghorn grip. He held it to one side, expectantly.

'Good boy.' Mason gave a sour grimace. 'Now put it on the boards real quietlike an' kick it over here 'less you wanna kiss goodbye to all you got.'

The doxie had regained the battered sofa and whispered, wide-eyed with fear, 'Do as he says, Jeb.'

Suddenly, Jeb saw his half-brother about to push through the batwing doors. 'Matt!' he screamed. 'Watch out!'

Mason swung to fire the Winchester at the incom-ing man, but as he did so, Jeb's Sidewinder crashed out and the gunman staggered, trying to hang on to the bar. Jeb fired again and blood spurted from Mason's chest as he hit the boards hard, his cheroot still gripped in his teeth.

Harold Hawkins pulled a razor-sharp scalping-knife from his boot and stabbed it hard into Abe's back as Seth began wildly firing shots from his Smith

& Wesson at the man half-through the batwing doors. The older bully had hauled a heavy 'hogleg' out from under his coat, but gave a wail of grief and his shot went wild, too, smashing the mirror behind Gus's head.

Matt Saunders's Peacemaker was in his grip, the seven-inch barrel spurting death, piercing Abe's guts to send him hurtling back into the fire.

Gus, the barkeep, ducked for cover and came up with his sawn-off twelve-guage splattering shots into Seth's chest, spinning him into eternity before he could fire a fifth bullet.

'Christ, Gus!' Jeb hollered, as pellets cut through his shirt sleeve. 'Put down that scattergun 'fore you kill us all.'

But he was mightily pleased with his performance, going over to the first man he had ever killed, yelling, 'Look at that, Matt. Right through the heart. Who said I couldn't shoot?'

'Yeah.' His older brother blew down the barrel of his smoking pistol, looking around warily. 'I'm obliged to you, Jeb. Who are they?'

'Three faggots who thought 'emselves hard cases.' Jeb kicked at Mason but it was like kicking a dead dog. He put another bullet in his head, jerked the cheroot from his clamped teeth and tossed it away.

'He ain't gonna be smoking no more of these.'

The thunder of the gunshots died away as suddenly as it had begun and as acrid blue smoke wafted across the saloon the occupants stared at the dead men on the floor and at the wounded Abe who was screaming as the flames from the logs licked at him.

'Yeah, don't like ya own medicine, do ya?' Jeb grinned and offered a hand. 'You want me to help ya out? Who sent you? Was it Vincent?'

Abe's face was agonized as he struggled to get up from the fireplace, his back and hair frizzling, but blood was already pumping from his back and gut. All he could do was nod and mutter, 'He promised . . . a thousand dollars.'

'Looks like you missed out, don't it?' Jeb shot him in the chest and he slumped back. 'Too bad, pal. So long.' The youth got to his feet and grinned. 'I gave him the *coup de grâce*, as they say. He'll be stoking them furnaces down below purty soon.'

'Yeah.' His half-brother was a man ten years older, slim and gaunt of face, black-haired, attired in a neat dark suit, a blue polkadot bandanna about his throat. 'Pull him outa the fire 'fore he stinks up this place.'

But old Harold was already doing that, dragging off Abe's boots. 'I'm gonna have his trousers and long pants, too, seein' as how he fried mine. Hee-haw!' He hooted with glee. 'Looks like he's got a nice li'l wad of greenbacks, too.'

'You earned 'em, oldtimer.' Jeb patted his bald head. 'You done well.'

'Aw, reminds me of that time the Sioux ambushed us out at Cherry Bluffs. . . .' Hawkins meandered on about some long-forgotten exploits. 'I'll have my knife back, too.'

The fallen angel, Alice, dressed in only pantalettes, stockings, slippers and a candystriped dressing gown, plus bangles and beads, giggled as she pointed to the half-naked Abe's withered little penis. 'He ain't got much on offer now, has he?'

'Hai-yee!' Jeb gave a triumphant whoop and hugged her to him triumphantly. 'You see the way I shot that main one, honey? Whoo-ee! He had no chance against me.'

'He was kinda distracted, wasn't he?' Matt Saunders said. 'Don't go kiddin' yourself you're some fast gun, Jeb. Because there's allus someone faster.'

'Aw, yeah, you would try to put me down wouldn't ya? I saved your damn life.'

'I've told you I'm beholden.' Matt picked up Mason's carbine. 'Nice Winchester. Latest model, '73.' He tossed it at his half-brother. 'You keep it.'

'To the victors the spoils,' Gus shouted, swiftly purloining Mason's fat wallet and Seth's gun. 'This nifty Smith & Wesson will do me. Help yourselves to whatever else they got, boys. Then sling 'em on my wagon out back and we'll bury 'em up on Boot Hill, though it's getting a tad overcrowded these days.'

Folks had come nosing in to see what all the noise was about, tut-tutting over the bodies on the floor. But a saloon shoot-out was no big deal in Washoe

City and they soon wandered off.

'A good mirror smashed, so I've helped myself to their leader's wallet. That OK, Mr Saunders? He owed for the brandy, too.'

'Sure.' Matt stroked his clean-shaven chin, deep in thought. 'Joshua Vincent sent 'em, did he? Sounds to me like I got a war on my hands, don't it?'

'Doncha worry, big brother.' Jeb slapped him on the back. 'You got me to look after you.'

'That's reassuring,' Matt murmured sarcastically, as he stood at the bar and the 'keep split the remains of the brandy between them.

'Aw, you worry too much, you ol' dongbeater,' Jeb yelled, still excited by the skirmish. 'Hot dang! I got cause to damn well celebrate. Yee-hoo!' he hollered, scooping up the saloon gal and whirling her around. 'C'm on, Alice, you got me all hotted up.'

As the youth stepped over the corpses and pools of blood with the girl in his arms towards the back room, Matt called out, 'Don't take too long. I'm headin' back to the ranch soon.'

Jeb ignored him, and as Gus met his grey eyes, Matt gritted out, 'If Joshua Vincent's sent out an assassination squad to get me he ain't gonna stop at that. Me, an' him, too, that crazy kid brother of mine, are gonna have to watch our backs.'

TWO

The sun was rising, flushing crimson the icy peaks of the Rockies as Joshua Vincent strode out on to the raised timber surround of the Tarantula ranch house and gazed out across the silvery green foothills of his domain, the wide butt-end of Gun Barrel Valley. Every inch as far as the eye could see belonged to him, Josh Vincent. And that was the way he intended it to stay. And more. He had a fierce urge to extend his holdings up along the northern barrel-end claimed by interloper Matt Saunders.

Suddenly he saw a rider approaching fast, quirting his pony hell for leather, splashing through the stream and swerving around the rocks of the valley and knots of cattle. The rancher's craggy face, beneath a mane of silvery hair, tensed. 'Looks like trouble,' he muttered.

When the cowboy galloped in, slid from the saddle of his sweating mount and gasped out his news,

Vincent cursed loudly and luridly, cursed the upstart Saunders and his whole damned outfit to hell.

He clattered back into his ranch house, snorting angrily into his bushy white moustache and glowering beneath bristling brows at his wife, Martha, who called, 'What's wrong, Josh? You sound like a bull with bellyache.'

'Ye'd be bellowin' if you heard what I've just heard.' Vincent scowled at his wife, his niece, Polly Vincent and his son, Grat, the burly spitting image of his daddy except that his bristly hair was black. They were all seated around the breakfast table. 'Three of my men gunned down by those Saunders and Riley bastards.'

'Josh, watch your language. Polly ain't used to this cussin'.'

'It'd make a saint cuss. Them two didn't give my boys a chance to speak out. Just shot 'em to hell, stole their cash, their guns, their hosses, even their boots an' pants.'

'Which boys?' Martha demanded. 'You mean three of our cowhands? Where? Out on the range?'

'Nah,' Vincent muttered, taking his seat back at the head of the table. 'Three other fellas I'd employed. Sent 'em into Washoe with a message for Matthew Saunders. Sounds like no sooner had they opened their mouths when they entered the saloon than they got set upon and ventilated.'

'He means riddled with holes,' Grat gruffly

18

explained, reaching to pat Polly's hand. 'Don't get upset, sweetie. These thangs happen out here.'

He glanced slyly at his father, for he had a good idea who his late *employees* had been and the reason for their mission. He pushed the remaining waffles and butter over as their Sioux maid brought in Vincent's platter of ham, eggs and tinned tomatoes. 'Sounds like your plan didn't go to plan, eh, Pa?'

'You keep outa this, Grat,' Vincent muttered, as he started stuffing the vittles into his mouth. 'Ain't nuthin' to do with you.'

'Sure it's to do with me. It's to do with all of us. Maybe you ain't aware what you're startin'. Range war once sparked can flare up like a forest fire. These may not be the last of your *employees* you lose.'

'What do you mean?' The dark-haired girl wiped her lips with her napkin and turned sage-green eyes on uncle. 'Is Grat saying you might have planned this violent encounter? It doesn't sound the sort of thing Mr Saunders would do without good reason. What is the cause of this trouble, might I know?'

'Don't you worry your head about it, Polly.' Grat patted her hand once again. 'These ain't your sedate St Louis circles.'

'We know the cause, OK,' Vincent growled. 'The Saunders mob have been cuttin' our wire and rustlin' our stock.'

'You sure about that?' Martha queried.

'Who the hell else would it be? They gotta be

taught a lesson.'

'Barbed wire's a big cause of contention in these parts, Polly,' Grat explained, as the girl tried to remove her hand from his bearlike paw.

Martha sighed deeply. 'I never thought to see Joshua Vincent stoop to its use. How we gonna get our cattle to Miles City if everybody puts up wire? Have you thought of that, Josh?'

'Stoop?' Vincent spluttered, his mouth full. 'What you talkin' about, woman?' he thundered, hammering the table with his fist so hard the delicate china rattled. 'I know what I'm doing. Am I the head of this household, or not?'

The slender Polly, in her velvet dress and clean lace collar, flushed, nervously. 'Matthew didn't strike me as a rustler or violent man. He seemed the epitome of a well mannered young gentleman, a rarity, it seems, out here.'

'Matthew?' It was Grat's turn to raise his voice. 'Since when have you been gittin' acquainted with Matthew Saunders?'

'When I last went into town. Aunt Martha was busy along at the grain store and I was getting groceries. The paper bag burst and stuff rolled all over the sidewalk. Matthew happened to be there and kindly helped me retrieve things. He walked me back to the wagon.'

'*Matthew*?' Grat boomed again. 'Huccome we ain't heard of this afore?'

'Possibly because I never mentioned it,' Polly rejoined. 'I wasn't aware I had to report on everybody I passed the time of day with.'

'Sounds like more than passing the time of day to me,' Grat shouted. 'Sounds like that wolf in sheep's clothing's been making eyes at you. I'm warning you—'

'Warning me?' Polly exclaimed. 'What do you mean?'

'Don't be fooled by Saunders's cool, handsome, gentlemanly exterior,' Martha intervened. 'Though I guess you ain't the only gal who has been. He ain't no gent. He's got a reputation, a history. He was some sorta fast gun up in the goldfields of Virginny City. The Vigilantes ran him outa there.'

'No. I don't believe it,' Polly replied. 'He seemed a very pleasant person to me.'

'Hell's fury!' Vincent got to his feet and hurled the remains of his breakfast plate at the wall, smashing it. 'Don't you understand English, gal? Matthew Saunders is a damned ruthless killer, a rustler who's no right to that land. Him and that no-good kid brother of his have murdered three of my men, cut my wire, rustled my cattle. He's a mad dog who's bared his teeth again.'

'Josh,' Martha shouted, 'there's no need for that.'

'You wimmin make me mad,' Vincent growled, buckling on his gunbelt. 'I tell ya, he's got to pay. They both have.'

21

Grat jumped to his feet, too, a worried look on his face, grabbing a carbine from the gunrack on the wall. His father was stomping out of the front door and Grat followed him, turning to shout, 'You better decide who's side you're on, Polly. Our'n or that snake in the grass.'

'Goodness, what gets into him?' Martha tut-tutted, as they helped the Sioux woman clean up the mess, and she met the girl's concerned eyes. 'You gotta stay away from Washoe City from now on, Polly. And git rid of any fancy feelin's you got for Matthew Saunders. You ever see him again you look the other way. This sounds bad.'

'But surely, if he has done what Uncle says he has, he will be given a fair trial to say his piece.'

'A fair trial?' Martha gave a twisted smile. 'Huh! They don't have no lawmen, no courts, no fair trials out here. The only law here is the law of the gun. It's a battle for survival. You better remember that, girl.'

THREE

Polly Vincent's father, Henry, had died of a sudden heart attack earlier that year, in April 1881, possibly brought on by his compulsive addiction to gambling. While Polly struggled with the upkeep of their dilapidated town house as well as minding their dry goods store, he spent most of his time and money in the St Louis casinos at the roulette wheel. Her mother had predeceased her husband several years before and perhaps it was just as well for it transpired that Henry Vincent was mired in vast debt. So Polly had found herself an orphan with barely enough cash in the till to pay for the funeral.

That had been a cold and mournful occasion. Beseiged by creditors Polly was at her wits' end to know what to do or how to repay them. Suddenly, like a tornado, Henry's brother Joshua had swept into her life He had arrived late on the riverboat, travelling all the way from his ranch in far off

Montana when he heard the news. His craggy face jutting from a mass of white hair and moustache, in his Stetson and frock coat, he immediately took charge.

'Your father was a lousy businessman and a born loser,' he opined in his loud gravelly tone. 'I warned him his gambling would be the ruin of him.'

'He just couldn't help it,' Polly said. 'It was like a disease.'

'That's true. Me an' him were as different as chalk and cheese. I'm a winner. What you gonna do now, gal?'

'I thought I might try to take in boarders here at the house and see if I can get the store back on its feet. But all these debts – it's going to take years to repay everybody.'

'Impossible,' Josh shouted, accustomed to being obeyed. 'Sell the house and the store. Then I'll settle what else there is to pay.'

He duly set the wheels in motion and the day after the auctions he sucked on a Havana cigar, sat in the house's one remaining armchair and finished off his brother's whiskey, stretching out his legs in his spurred boots. 'Be thankful ye're rid of this millstone about your neck. You're free of debt now. What do ye plan to do?'

'I've applied for a position as a governess. I'm quite good with children,' the girl began, tentatively. 'It would at least give me somewhere to live.'

'Yeah, an' not much else.' Joshua appraised the pretty 19-year-old. 'That's no life for a young gal.'

Montana was woman-poor country. Many men ended up marrying or living with a fallen angel, as the saloon whores were called, or with an Indian squaw. A respectable, well-mannered filly like Polly would be quite a prize out there. And Josh had his son Grat in mind.

'Hey, I've an idea,' he roared. 'I'll settle up your affairs and we'll hightail it back to the ranch.'

'But—'

'No, doncha worry your purty li'l head. Ye'll be welcomed as one of the family.'

So Polly had found herself aboard the shallow-draught paddle boat *Josephine*, heading up the Missouri River past Kansas City and on up to Council Bluffs where Joshua Vincent stood beneath the tall stack belching smoke and declaimed, 'This is where I set out with a wagon train thirty years ago heading West across the Kansas plains towards the Rockies. That was 'fore the Injin wars begun an' the buff' herds stretched as far as the eye could see.'

'Do you get any trouble from the tribes these days in Montana?' she asked, somewhat nervously.

'Hell no, like the buff' most of 'em's been wiped out or put on reservations. After that idjit Custer got hisself and his boys ambushed, most of the warring tribes been blown to smithereens by the army's how-itzers. 'Course, there's still a few hostiles and hoss thieves about but we know how to handle 'em.'

'Goodness. Poor things!'

'Aw, ye'll be seein' plenty tame Injins but most have had the fight knocked outa them.'

As the *Josephine* churned steadily on its way up past Sioux City and headed beneath gloomy overcast skies through the dreary flatlands of Dakota, and as they tied up at some desolate cabin to take on wood, Polly did, indeed, see several parties of wandering Indians, huddled in their blankets on their stunted ponies, watching them as if from another world. Yes, she thought, they look like a defeated people.

Evenings in the steamer's saloon were jolly, with after dinner high jinks; two officers returning to Fort Keogh playing piano and singing ballads and trying to persuade her to dance.

The captain, Grant Marsh, was a legend in his own lifetime for he had in '73 pushed the *Josephine* through shallows and sandbanks a record 483 miles up the Yellowstone as far as Hell Roaring Rapids. And three years later he had taken off injured from the Rosebud after the Custer defeat.

At Bismarck the North Pacific Railroad had resumed operations and was laying track on the west side of the Missouri. It had been brought to a halt in '73 due to Indian attacks.

'Soon there's gonna be a track all the way from Chicago to Miles City,' Captain Marsh mused. 'And that ain't gonna be good news for us packet boats nor the mule trains.'

'No,' Joshua Vincent whooped, 'but it's sure gonna be welcomed by us cattlemen.'

On the *Josephine* ploughed, leaving the wide Missouri and heading up the turbulent Yellowstone, past Stanley Stockade and the wide mouth of the Powder River. Their more than a thousand mile journey was through when they tied up at the landing stage at Miles City.

'Welcome to the last outpost of civilization,' Joshua chuckled, as he led Polly down the gangplank. 'Albeit the main cause of death in this place is from whiskey or lead pizening.'

Polly eyed the dismal collection of backstreets behind a vast pile of buffalo skins waiting to be shipped back down river. At the entries to dance halls, saloons and parlour houses painted doxies were hanging around the doors, wild screams emanating from within and a man staggered out to fall face first into the mud.

It didn't look much like civilization to her.

'Town was flooded when I come through,' Joshua yelled. 'Tongue River bust its banks with the spring snow melt. You needed a rowboat to git across Main Street. Come on. Here it is.'

Polly screamed as as she sank knee-deep into the ooze and tried to follow him across as a cursing, whip-cracking 'skinner, driving a dozen pair of oxen hauling the Diamond D double-wagon bore down on her. She scrambled out of the way of the steaming beasts.

Away from the log cabin stores and false fronts stood the imposing McQueen House, newly built by a southern gentleman, Colonel McQueen, where wealthy ranch owners wintered. Polly floundered on to the sidewalk and up its steps, trying to wipe some of the mud from her boots and long skirts. There was a cattleman's convention in sway and the hotel was packed, so they had to share a poky room up among the third floor attics.

'They don't have elevators in this civilized town?' Polly remarked, as she hauled her carpet bag up the narrow stairs.

'Elevators? What are them?'

'The new Otis Elevator. In St Louis you step inside and they whisk you up six floors.'

'This ain't St Louis,' her uncle grunted, as he rigged up a blanket over a rope between their two bunks to give her some privacy.

'And you don't have hip baths in the rooms, I see.'

'Only bath house is behind the barber shop along the street,' Joshua replied. 'The maid'll bring some hot water for the hand basin if you want a wash.'

He was sticking nuggets of wood into a tin stove. 'Gotta git this lit so we don't lose our fingers or toes to frostbite in the night.'

Polly wasn't sure whether he was joking or not – it wasn't *that* cold – but she certainly couldn't fault the

28

food in the crowded dining room: an extensive menu including soups, oysters, fresh-caught salmon and trout, roasts of mutton, venison, buffalo loin or elk with dishes of steaming vegetables, celery and sweet potatoes, followed by a choice of pastries and fruit pies, rounded off with coffee and doughnuts if you were still peckish.

'Lieutenant Peabody invited me out to the social at the fort tomorrow night,' she remarked. 'Can we go?'

'Aw, no, we gotta catch the stage to Junction City in the marnin',' her uncle said. 'We still got a helluva way to go.'

He didn't tell her that he'd had a private word with Peabody and his pal outside their cabin on the *Josephine* and told them to keep their lustful eyes off his neice. 'She's already spoken for,' he had growled, tapping his revolver butt. 'Git my meaning?'

An officer's remuneration and quarters at the fort certainly weren't to be sneezed at. And Vincent didn't want her to be targeted by any of their ilk, or the snooty English remittance men, wealthy ranchers or drunken millionaires who hung around this outpost. So before he went out that night to look up his friend Tiger Lily at a certain 'parlour house' he ordered Polly to stay in the room and not to talk to any men because there were some 'rough, chiselling varmints around and gunplay wasn't out of the question'.

29

'Goodness!' Polly exclaimed, as she kept the stove fizzing and listened to some extremely raucous conversation through the thin pine-board walls of men in adjacent rooms. 'It's enough to make a girl blush. But most enlightening. So that's what they talk about!'

'Keep your voices down,' Joshua roared, when he came in at midnight. 'There's some respectable ladies in this hotel tryin' to git some shut-eye.' At which he fell asleep, snoring lustily.

FOUR

Polly was up early for breakfast in the hotel dining room. She overheard Colonel McQueen say that the social at Fort Keogh that night had been cancelled due to the death of a Captain Hale, of the 7th Cavalry, in a skirmish with hostile Sioux. The officers and their ladies were much distressed, flags were at half-mast and there would be a memorial service.

Polly went outside to view the frontier scene, so different to St Louis. A delivery wagon was being driven along the muddy main street by a soldier and to her surprise, as it passed her, an Indian in full eagle-feather war bonnet, fringed leggings and beaded moccasins, suddenly slipped from beneath its canvas cover and darted into Huffman's photographic studio.

'Gracious!' Polly said to herself. 'Should I call for help?'

Perplexed, she peeped into the doorway and hissed to a thin hawkfaced man, 'I was wondering . . .

31

an Indian. . . .'

'That's OK, my dear,' the photographer, Mr Huffman said. 'The driver sneaked him out of the fort. He'll take him back in an hour or so. He's a prisoner there. Keep it under your hat.'

'Oh, I see,' Polly replied, although she was not sure she did.

'Do you want to meet him? Come in.' Huffman beckoned her into a back room where stood the Sioux warrior in all his finery, a bear claw necklace around his throat, various gewgaws decorating a striped kind of blanket-coat and a scalping knife in a beaded sheath dangling from his belt. He stared at her haughtily, his high-cheekboned face like polished, sculpted bronze.

'This is Eta Ma Gozua or Rain in the Face. I'm trying to get pictures of these fellows before all the Old West is swept away. They are allowed to wander around inside the fort but General Miles don't allow them into town. Rain in the Face was in the thick of the fighting at Little Big Horn. Some say he cut out Custer's heart, but he denies that.'

'Oh dear. Isn't he dangerous? Won't he try to escape?'

'No, he's surrendered, given his word not to.' Huffman ducked under a black cover behind his camera. 'Excuse me, I must get on.'

'Yes, me too,' Polly called. 'I've got to catch the stage.'

Billings, a hundred miles on, was just another wide street bordered by shabby cabins, saloons and stores. Her uncle had two horses waiting for them at the livery. 'You know how to ride, doncha?'

A bunch of cowboys on a corral fence grinned as she tried to get on an ornery bay. Joshua gave her a leg-up and she perched precariously side-saddle.

'Ain't no need trying to look ladylike. Hitch ya skirt up and sling a leg over,' Joshua growled.

Polly tugged at her clothing and managed to do so when a gunshot exploded; the bronco leapt and, to the whoops of the onlookers, set off at a gallop out of town. Polly hung on to the saddle horn, her feet losing the stirrups. The saddle began to slide to one side. She jerked hard on the only rein she had in her left hand. Thundering along at full gallop, the bay wheeled to the right. Polly parted company. She went flying through the air like a tossed pancake and landed flat on her back.

Joshua charged up, caught the bay and cantered back to her. 'What the hell ya trying to do to my hoss?' he hollered. 'Thought you said you could ride.'

Winded, unable to move, she heard only a weird gurgle emanating out of her. When she got her breath back and was on her feet, she pointed at Joshua and back at the cowboys. 'You all did that on purpose.'

'I'll settle with those guys another day.' Josh tightened the cinch. 'C'mon, git back on.' He smiled to himself. 'Must say, I forgot this bay's a tad gunshy.'

'Huh!' Polly said, when she was on board. 'Just because he's back in his home territory he's trying to humiliate me.'

But Joshua wasn't listening, setting a hard pace, putting his horse to a lope across a desolate plain beneath grey louring skies that seemed to stretch on into infinity.

It was true. The old patriarch's attitude had suddenly become more bullying. Polly's bones and backside ached as she strove all day to stay on her mount.

Joshua barely paused as they passed the bloody carcasses of about fifty bison scattered on the plain. A greasy-looking skinner was loading their 'robes' on to his horse and cart.

Joshua didn't deign to greet him. 'They've wiped out nearly all of 'em on the southern plains. Now they're starting on the northern ones.'

'Don't they take any of the meat?' she asked.

'Nah! Might take a tongue or slice of hump, but mostly they leave it all to rot.'

On they went with Polly pounding along behind until darkness began to overshadow them. Suddenly they saw a firelight ahead, flickering. 'Goodness!' the girl wondered. 'Are they Indians?'

Joshua rode on and hollered, 'Hello, the camp!'

It was a party of hunters returning to Billings with their catch. Butchered antelope and hugely-antlered elk were hanging from trestles nearby. Polly clambered from her horse with relief. And, as she was as hungry as a hunter herself, she didn't refuse the platter of crisply-roasted tenderloin of elk they passed her. 'You're just in time for supper, miss,' one said.

That night was her first taste of sleeping out on the prairie rolled up in a blanket by the fireside. In the morning they headed on. Craggy, pine-girt hills had suddenly appeared out of the mist.

'These are the Crazy Mountains,' Joshua shouted, heading his mustang up through a pass. 'Ain't far now.'

At noon they reached a verdant, green-swooping valley amid the grey rocks, and not far off loomed the icy fangs of the Rockies. Polly had little time to admire the scene before a bunch of completely wild cowboys on half-wild mustangs came whooping up.

'Meet the boys,' Joshua said. 'Welcome to the Tarantula Ranch.'

Her Aunt Martha and Cousin Grat did, indeed, make her welcome that first week. But the Vincents's 16-year-old daughter, Harriet, treated her with lofty contempt as a tenderfoot from the hated East.

A true tomboy, the tousle-haired Harriet strutted around in shotgun chaps, a brace of pistols on her hips. But it was mid-April, the spring round-up had begun and more often than not she was out on the range with the men.

Polly herself quickly realized that she would be expected to pull her weight; a woman's tasks were multifarious around a ranch. There was the laundry, bed-making, cooking, water-fetching, hens to feed, eggs to collect, bread to bake and today, after that ugly scene with Uncle Joshua, a broom to get to help the Sioux woman clean up the mess.

Pausing in her task, Polly looked out of the window and saw Joshua Vincent apparently arguing with his son Grat out by the corral. Grat! That was another problem. He had started making advances towards her, placing his hairy hand on hers – and other parts of her anatomy – at any opportunity. Polly had a sinking sensation that as well as being an unpaid skivvy, soon she would be expected to marry the 'son and heir' and be for the rest of her life his bed-warmer and baby-producer. She shuddered at the thought. The simple fact was, she just didn't fancy him.

FIVE

'Have you thought this through, Pa?' Grat asked, as they headed towards the corral. 'Aincha bitin' off more than you can chew?'

'You go tell Dusty and the boys to tool up and saddle up and be ready to earn their thirty-a-month for once in their lives. Tell 'em to check their weapons and powder. We're gonna need every gun we got.'

'Pa, tell me the truth.' Grat blocked his father's way, his dark eyes pleading with him. 'What's going on? Did you really send those gunmen to kill Saunders? Why you so set on putting up wire all of a sudden? We've allus hated it, like Ma says.'

'Yeah, I sent 'em. Kill them rats once and for all. But seems like the rat-catchers weren't no dang use, so we gotta do it ourselves. Wire, yeah, sure I hate it. Doncha see, boy? It's just a temporary ruse. We cut off Saunders's entry and exit from the valley, he ain't gonna be able to get his cattle out to market. They'll have to go across the hills.'

'Aw,' Grat mused, stroking his jaw, 'I see. But I still gotta say, this all sounds a tad crazy to me. We were gettin' along with 'em easy enough up to now.'

'Chris'sakes!' the old patriarch yelled. 'Doncha understand? They got no right to that end of the valley. They're interlopers. It belongs to me.'

'But, Pa,' Grat wailed. 'Do we need more land like that? It's high, rocky, a lot of snow?'

His father caught him by his neckerchief, glowering into his face. 'You call yourself a son of mine? You go do what you're told and hurry it up. And be prepared to fight, boy.'

Joshua Vincent, Grat and fifteen of his rough and ready ranch-hands rode hard towards Washoe City and wheeled into the main street, hauling in outside the saloon.

'Dusty!' Vincent gritted out to his wiry foreman. 'Bring in three of the boys. The rest of ya stay outside and be on your toes. This ain't no birthday party.'

His long white hair hanging down to his shoulders from beneath his tall black hat, his black frock coat flapping in the breeze, Vincent gripped the butt of his old, blued Colt .45 on his hip and pushed through the batwing doors into the bar room, a wild look in his hollows of eyes. His men around him, he checked to make sure there was no threat from those there and strode to the bar.

'Hear tell you had a hand in killin' three of my men,' he thundered at the landlord, Gus Brown.

'Didn't know they were your men, Mr Vincent,' Gus replied, wiping the bar with a rag. 'Just seemed like three troublemakers. One of 'em insulted me, spat in my face, the other two tortured poor ol' Harold over the fire. When they pulled their guns we had to put 'em down.'

'Mad dogs gotta be put down,' Harold Hawkins hooted from his chair by the log fire. 'I'm proud to say I helped out.'

'Yeah, you thievin', traitorous bastards did all right for yourselves, didn't ya? That was my cash you stole from those boys.'

'Aw, the two who scorched my pants didn't have much on 'em,' Harold hollered. 'Nuthin' more than a few dollars. I figured they owed me that.'

'That means the other'n, Mason, musta been carrying my five hundred dollars I entrusted to him.' Joshua turned back to barkeep Brown, who wiped his hands uncomfortably, 'Guess you thought your murderous assault had come up trumps, eh, Gus? I'll give you five seconds to hand it over.'

'There weren't that much,' Gus demurred, eyeing his visitors uneasily. 'What proof you got it's yourn, anyhow, Mr Vincent?'

'Proof? They were my men carrying my money. It ain't none of your business why.' The rancher grabbed Brown's close-cropped head and brought it down to smash on the counter. 'Don't argue with me. Get my wallet.'

'Aagh!' Gus's forehead had hit a glass and there was a mess of blood on his face. 'This ain't fair,' he moaned, as he groped towards the till, unlocked it and produced the wallet.

Vincent took it from him, checked the contents, tucked it in his pocket and said, 'That's better. Now serve us all a whiskey.'

Brown mopped at his face looking more than sorry for himself and filled six tumblers from a whiskey bottle. 'That's two dollars.'

'Take it from what you stole from my wallet.' As the men reached for their drinks, Joshua Vincent muttered, 'Let that be a lesson to you, Gus. You better decide whose side you're on.'

'I ain't on nobody's side. I'm just trying to do my job.'

'In future, if you wanna stay healthy, you will do business only with me and my boys and' – he glowered at the drinkers and card players silently watching – 'and allow in here only townspeople who are loyal to me. The Saunders bunch and any scum who support or do trade with them, will not be welcome in this hostelry.'

'I can't do that,' Gus stuttered. 'Jeb Riley is a good customer here, so are the Longbranch cowhands. I need their custom to survive.'

'Looks like you'll have to survive without 'em, don't it?' Vincent strolled over to the log fire, kicked at a log, making sparks spritz out. 'It sure would be easy for this place to burn down. These timber walls are tinder dry.'

'This isn't right,' the corpulent owner of the town's general store, Horace Poulson, put in, rising from his seat at a poker game. 'Coming in here, beating up Gus, making threats like that.'

'This applies to you, too, Poulson, you fat, cheatin' bag of wind,' the rancher shouted. 'Whose side are *you* on? Mine? If so, you will do no more trade with the Saunders mob.'

'That's ridiculous,' Poulson fumed. 'You can't threaten the whole town.'

'Can't we?' Grat had decided it was time to give his father support. He picked a glowing brand out of the fire, ambled over to the portly trader and waved it dangerously close to his rosy nose, making him flinch back. 'If this saloon caught fire, you know, I reckon the whole town would be engulfed in flames. A terrible thing, fire is.'

'Gentlemen, we have no wish to harm you or your livelihoods,' Joshua Vincent cried out. 'But until this matter is settled I will need to know where your loyalties lie.'

He tossed back the liquor with a grimace of his craggy jaws, and led his men back out of the saloon. 'Come on,' he shouted to the waiting cowhands,

'We've got work to do. We gotta get that barbed wire fence back up.'

In her shotgun chaps and fringed buckskin jacket Harriet came charging in from the prairie on her spirited skewbald, her Long Tom buffalo rifle held in one hand, rested across the horse's neck. She leapt from the saddle and went at full tilt up the steps to the porch and crashed open the front door. 'What's going on?' she yelled. 'Where's everybody gawn? Where's Pa?'

'Lawks, girl!' her mother cried. 'You make more clatter and commotion than your father. Where've you been? You missed breakfast.'

'I been out on the range lookin' fer them lousy rustlers. They'll sure know it if they meet me. I asked a question, Ma. Where are the men?'

'They went to Washoe City on men's business. It ain't no concern of our'n. Why don' you put that rifle aside? It's much too heavy for a gal.'

Harriet brandished the long-barrelled Springfied. 'I can do anythang a man can do and better. This rifle's accurate at nearly a mile. You ain't gonna see me toting one of them prissy lady's sporting rifles.'

As, at that point, Polly came from the kitchen, she added, scornfully, 'Maybe you should git one of them girlie thangs for *her*. But not fer me. What kinda business they gawn on? Killin' business? They mighta waited fer me.'

'I came to ask if you wanted a coffee, Harriet?'

'Yeah, sure, Polly put the kettle on. That's about all you Eastern gals are good fer.'

'You don't have to be so rude. I'm quite aware that housework is beneath you.'

'Yes, watch your tongue, young lady. Try to be nice to your cousin.'

'Huh! Her and her fancy airs. Seems to think it's us who's beneath *her*. So why they gone to Washoe City?'

'Your father believes it's Matthew Saunders who's behind the wire cutting and rustling.'

'Matthew?' Harriet cried. 'He wouldn't do that sorta thang.'

She might dress and act like a troublesome young cowboy, but Harriet had a heart of a lovestruck teenage girl when it came to the tall, handsome and mostly silent – towards her – rancher who lived at the far end of the valley.

'And that reminds me,' she growled, as Polly returned from the kitchen with a steaming mug of coffee. 'Hear tell you've been makin' cow eyes at Matt.' She jerked the dangerous end of the rifle at the girl. 'We better git one thang straight. He ain't fer you.'

'For your information I don't make cow eyes at men.' Polly plonked the coffee on to a table, spilling it. 'And I don't take orders as to who, and who not, I should speak to. I've already had your brother trying to lay down the law to me about Mr Saunders this morning. Seems like the gossips in this vicinity are pretty quick at stirring things up.'

'Yeah, we don't miss much.'

'You both got to forget that fella,' Martha shrilled. 'He ain't no good for either of ya.'

'So what are you going to *do* if I should speak to Mr Saunders, might I ask?'

'That's simple. If you do' – Harriet cocked the rifle and swung it to aim at Polly's head – 'I'll blow your dang brains out.'

Martha erupted with a burst of scoffing laughter. 'Harriet sure knows how to win an argument.'

Polly eyed the girl coolly. 'Yes, well, maybe I don't find it so funny.'

When she returned to the kitchen, the Indian woman, Pretty Nose, gave her a downturned grimace as if they were both unwilling hostages of this family.

'You better take care, missy,' she said. 'That gal crazy 'nuff do what she say.'

Polly shook her head and went back to kneading dough for their bread hitting it hard with her fists. Yes, she did feel like a prisoner. She had no way of even getting back to Miles City, let alone St Louis. She was destitute. All the funds raised from the sale of the house and store had gone to repay creditors, or so Uncle Joshua had said.

Was she to be trapped in this house, subject to the

whims of this family for eternity? Was there no way of escape?

SIX

As the snow cleared and the mountain slopes greened over it was time at the Longbranch ranch, too, for the spring round-up, one of the most hectic times of the year.

Matthew Saunders and his men were up before dawn and set out to probe the creeks and gullies of the Crazy Mountains to bring in their half-wild long-horns.

Matt scraped a stick in the mud as a rough map to show which area they would rake through that day, and the chuck wagon was sent on ahead to meet them at the appointed spot where they would bring in the stock for branding.

'Jeb, you and Curly scour Wolf Creek. Me and Dave will take the box canyon.' He paired off the rest of his eight cow-punchers. 'We all meet back at the river. That clear enough? Right, vamoose!'

He watched the men choose mounts from the

remuda. 'They're honest enough and loyal, but they ain't gun-slingers,' he said to young Jeb. 'If it comes to a battle with Vincent and his bunch we're out-numbered two to one. So stay away from their wire. Don't give 'em any cause or excuse to attack.'

'Where's your spirit, big brother?' Jeb yelled. 'You're as nervous as some old dame. What's the matter? You past it? You gave them vigilantes up at Virginia City a run for their money. You protected our family and avenged your pa. Hell, you used to be a hero of mine, real fast gun. What's wrong? You lost your nerve?'

'Can't you get it into your skull, Jeb? We're in a very dangerous situation. In my opinion Joshua Vincent won't be content until he's wiped our outfit off the map.'

'Yeah, well, in *my* opinion,' Jeb replied, 'that old fool Vincent has had it his own way far too long. What makes him think he owns the whole of the valley? We'll just have to show him he's wrong. And in my further opinion the best way to do that is to hire us some extra guns too.'

'Maybe you're right. Maybe it's the only way.' Matt stroked his thin jaw. 'But first we gotta git these cows counted and calves branded, so let's go.'

It was true, Joshua Vincent had no God-given right to the whole of the valley. Certainly, he was one of the original settlers on the frontier and had claimed the best land in that area. Matthew realized that he was a latecomer and considered himself lucky to have gotten the upper part of the valley. Joshua had shown no wish to run him off when he first arrived. Why should he now?

'Well,' he said, 'I'm only doing what every other rancher has done, grabbed land from the poor damn Indians and asserted that it is now mine. I guess we have got to fight to hang on to it, same as everyone else.'

'You're sure durn tooting,' Jeb yelled. 'At last ye're talkin' sense.'

Matt had little time to think about his problems – or for that matter the delectable Polly Vincent – as they rode up through the thorn brush and dense choke cherries, at the ready with their lariats to deal with any wild cow who took exception to them rousting out her and her calves. If she charged, swinging those vicious long horns, their riposte would be to rope her and make her hit the dust.

Matt was dressed for the work in leather jacket and chaps, his flat-brimmed hat pulled down over his brow. They worked their way up through the canyon flushing out the stock and by noon had herded a good bunch of the angry beasts back out and had them headed to the meeting point.

'You done well, boys,' Matt shouted, as he surveyed the milling mob of beeves. 'At a rough guess I'd say there's more'n a thousand head.'

Hot coffee and crackers were being handed out by

the cook at his chuck wagon to give the boys a brief
break; the branding irons were in the fire. Fresh
horses were chosen from the remuda into which had
been put the three ill-treated mustangs on which the
would-be killers had arrived at Washoe City. The lush
mountain pasture would soon work wonders for
them.

Matt whistled for his favourite cutting horse,
Crackers, so named because of his fondness for the
hardtack biscuits, and he quickly trotted over to
claim his treat as a saddle was thrown over his back.
He had been specially trained for roping and cutting
cows and calves from the main herd and was so alert
and intelligent Matt hardly had need of the reins.
For the rest of the afternoon he let Crackers do his
work.

As soon as Matt had pointed out the one he
wanted Crackers' ears would twitch and his eyes
would be glued on it. As soon as the longhorn was
singled out to the edge, it would make a sudden
wheel to try to get back in among the mob again. But
Crackers would be in between the animal and the
herd so it couldn't get back in. It would try dodging
and spurting for freedom but Crackers anticipated
every move and often sent the dogeys running in the
right direction with a nip at their backsides.

When the fleeing beast was close enough to the
fire, if it were a calf Matt would rope it by its back
legs, drag it across and jump down to apply his LB

brand to sizzle its hide. If it were a steer it had to be head-roped and grappled to the earth.

It was hard, dangerous work amid the clouds of dust. In the hurly-burly men went crashing to the ground with their horses or were pulled from the saddle. If he were unlucky, a man could be gored or lose a finger trapped in a taughtened rope. Luckily, by nightfall and after a fifteen-hour day, they were all in one piece. While five men tucked into sowbelly and potato stew the other five patrolled the perimeter of the herd and would take shifts to do so through the night.

When they came in at midnight from their stint, Matt and Jeb filled their tin coffee mugs and settled down on their soogans beside the blazing camp-fire. The herd had settled down, and but for a mournful bellow now and again, the yipping of coyotes and the distant howl of a wolf pack, all was peaceful under the stars.

'So,' Dave drawled, as he carefully rolled a cigarette. 'Is the talk true, Matt? Jeb says you were some sorta fast-gun in Virginia City.'

'Sure it's true,' Jeb cried. 'Matt gunned down one by one the men who killed his pa. Shot each one in fair combat.'

'Hang on a minute. Jeb was only a toddler. He don't know the ins and outs of it.' Matthew Saunders did not like speaking about his past but it seemed he had to explain. 'The fact is my father and mother

50

and me, just a toddler too in them days, arrived in a covered wagon at Alder Creek in the early '60s. That's where the stampede was; thousands of men scrabbling for gold in a ten-mile stretch.'

'Yeah,' Jeb put in. 'Ten million dollars in dust and nuggets was taken outa that valley before it come to an end.'

'From what I gathered we never did too well until one day when I was about ten we hit paydirt. All I remember was a bunch of men arriving and demanding we hand over the claim. Pa argued, went for his gun and they shot him down in cold blood. After burying him Ma and I moved into Virginia City.'

'And vowed vengeance,' Jeb prompted.

Matt frowned at him. 'You gonna let me tell this?'

'Sure, go on.'

'What was a woman to do? That was a hard, crude city, as cold-hearted as those grey mountains all around. There were shootings every day in the saloons. The sheriff, Henry Plummer, secretly ran a gang of road agents who preyed on gold consignments. It's said they killed more than a hundred men in their time. Anyway Ma eventually married Jeb's father, a wild, hard-drinking Irishman. A year later Jeb was born. He'll probably agree it wasn't the best of times, that one-room shack we lived in.'

'Yeah,' Jeb agreed. 'Pa believed in bringing kids up tough.'

'Yeah, we all suffered some of his kicks and curses

when he was in his cups.'

'So tell 'em how you waited, practising your shootin', waiting to take your revenge.'

Matthew sighed. 'It all festered in my mind. I knew who those men were. I saw them around town. By the time I was fifteen some honest men had secretly organized vigilantes and one by one Plummer and his gang were hanged by their necks. What I didn't know was that Pa's killers were members of that masked vigilante group.'

'Matt stalked every one of his pa's killers, gunned them down. Then he had to run for his life otherwise he would have been found hanging from a telegraph pole too.'

'That's more or less the way it was,' Matthew said. 'I'd been hunting game most my young life and was a pretty good shot. I was wild and obsessed, but I was lucky. I killed those five men. I ain't proud of it now, I was lucky I got out.'

'Aw, you did what you had to do. You were on a righteous mission. Folks still talk about it. Then when Ma died I was about fourteen. My old man was a hopeless drunk, so I tracked down Matt and came and joined him.'

'Yep,' Matthew smiled, enigmatically. 'It was a bit of a surprise, I must say. OK, boys, let's get a coupla hours sleep, shall we?'

'Very interesting, Matt,' Dozy Dave, as they called him, drawled. He lay back on his saddle and pulled his hat over his eyes to blot out the moonglow. 'All those killings. Now we know why you're such a miserable cuss.'

SEVEN

Grat Vincent tugged at his heavy black moustache, uncomfortable as he leaned his bulk against a kitchen cupboard and watched Polly at her cooking chores. Every time she bent down to poke the grate of the iron oven he was overcome with lascivious imaginings to do with the shadowy shape of her back-side beneath the baggy working skirt. Finally he could bear it no more. He stepped forward and groped for her with one of his huge hands, pulling her into him with the other. Polly screamed and dropped the tray of hot biscuits with a clatter. 'Let go,' she hissed. 'Let me be!'

'I can't help it, Polly,' he groaned into her ear, hanging on to her. 'I'm crazy about ya. You don't know what you do to me.'

'I can guess,' she said, grimly. 'You don't leave much to the imagination.'

'I'm not such a bad guy,' he whined, in his nasal

sing-song 'One of these days when the old man's gone I'll be a rich ranch-owner in my own right. I'm tellin' ya, Polly, you could do worse than me.'

He had quit exploring and now had his fingers entwined across her belly holding her firm. Polly tried to unbuckle the fat hairy things with her own hands but he had her tight. 'You're my cousin,' she pleaded. 'This isn't right.'

'Aw, we don't worry about thangs like that in these parts,' he gurgled, as his mother's voice called out, 'What's going on?'

Grat let her go and Polly knelt down to retrieve the biscuits as Martha bustled in. 'I dropped the tray,' she said. 'It was hot.'

Her aunt gave Grat a look and grinned. 'Has my boy bin botherin' ya? Waal, he cain't help it if you go flouncing around like you do. She's a mighty purty gal, ain't she, Grat?'

'Yurrrr, she is,' Grat mumbled. 'I jest cain't keep my eyes offen her.'

'Or his hands,' Polly added.

It was true. Just the sight of her naked elbows as Polly was rolling the pastry made him come over all queasy.

'Polly's a lady, Grat. She comes from civilized St Louis. She's read books and larned how to play the py-anny. You gotta treat her right, boy.'

Polly regained her feet with the biscuits. 'I'd prefer you didn't discuss me as if I'm some slave standing on the auction block. Perhaps you'd like to examine my teeth at the same time?'

'Come on, honey,' Aunt Martha coaxed. 'It's time you quit all these hoity-toity airs. They don't rub up too well out here. Waal, I guess you must know we're all agreed you'll make a fine wife fer Grat and we'd be glad to have ya in the family. So what's your complaint? What'n hail else ya gonna do?'

'I don't wish to appear rude or ungrateful, Aunt,' Polly replied, brushing a stray lock of hair from her eyes. 'I'm sure Grat will make some lucky girl an admirable husband, but it's not going to be me.'

'Why's that?' Grat demanded. 'You think you're too damn good for me?'

'No.' Polly wrinkled her nose, shook her head in exasperation. 'Don't you see, Grat? You're a nice guy but I just don't find you attractive that way.'

'So?' Martha picked up the rolling pin and slapped it in her palm, threateningly. 'What sort of man do you fancy – Matthew Saunders by any chance?'

'No,' Polly lied. 'I've never really thought about it. But' – out of devilment she couldn't resist adding – 'I do prefer a man with a slimmer physique. And one who keeps his hands to himself.'

'You cheeky bitch,' Martha cried. 'After all we've done fer you.'

'I'm sorry. I didn't mean to upset you. It's just that a heavy, hirsute man is not for me. That's all.'

'Ha!' Martha smashed the rolling pin on the table as if she'd like to smack it around Polly's head. 'Maybe if we kicked you out, let you try an' make your way in Washoe City you'd soon change your mind. Har! Most gals thar end up with a bun in their oven and no ring on their finger.'

'Ma, shut up,' Grat warned. 'Polly ain't goin' nowhere.'

'Fergit her, Grat.' Aunt Martha swept from the kitchen, calling out, 'The ungrateful hussy. She ain't no right in this house.'

'I wish you wouldn't all make me feel so guilty.' Polly sniffled, almost in tears. 'I can't help it.'

'Forget it.' Grat gently chucked her under the chin and bent forward to kiss her lips. Polly jerked her head away, the kiss brushing her cheek. 'Don't cry, sweetheart. Don't worry about Ma. She'll come round. And' – he grinned – 'so will you.'

Left alone, Polly blew her nose, stubbornly, hanging on to her pride. But it was a cold frightening wilderness out there. What if Matt did not want her? How could she make it on her own?

Jeb Riley and his sidekick Curly rode over a rocky spur of the Crazy Mountains and sent their mustangs careering down through a cliff of loose shale.

At the bottom were the newly hammered-in posts of Vincent's barbed wire, which stretched off in a straight line across the pasture to the opposite hill.

'Them bastards been busy agin, ain't they?' Jeb chuckled, pulling a pair of wire cutters from his saddle-bag. 'Time to clip their wings.'

'Matt ain't gonna like it.' Curly watched, dubiously, as Jeb jumped down and cut wire springing back from first one, then several more posts. From the top of the cliff they had checked to make sure the coast was clear, but Curly scanned the horizon again nervously. 'Hurry it up, Jeb, for Gawd's sake. That'll do. There's plenty of space to get through.'

His hat hanging on his back, he was younger than Jeb, about fifteen, and as the harsh prairie wind swept his curly mop over his eyes he scratched it back. 'Thought you said we was just going into town for some fun.'

'Aw, you're a worse ol' croaker than Matt.' The irrascible, ginger-headed Jeb dragged the wire aside with his gloved hands, swung back on his bronco and pointed towards a bunch of heifers on Vincent's side of the fence. 'Those'll do fer us. Let's git 'em.'

'What?' But the impressionable Curly was well accustomed to the boss's brother's erratic behaviour, so he spurred his pony spurting after him, excited too by their bravado. 'Yee-hagh!' he yelled as they rounded up the dogies.

'We'll take 'em along to Wild Cat canyon.' Jeb had a small branding iron in his saddle-bag. 'We'll burn LB on to their hides then take 'em into town for old Sam the butcher to slaughter. He'll be glad of a bit of fresh meat on the cheap. It'll give us a packet of spending money, boy. We're gonna have a rip-roaring time.'

Jeb cracked his lariat end at the heifers and sent them trotting on their way, tails high. He warbled a stirring rebel song as they cantered along: 'I'm riding in the cause of Liberty . . . I'm ridin' to set my country free. . . .' as if he hadn't got a care in the world.

'Where's Jeb got to?' Matthew sang out, as he left their cabin after breakfast and strolled over to the low-slung soddy bunkhouse, smoke trickling from its chimney.

The boys were turning out for the day's work, Dozy Dave among them, who eyed Matt and drawled with his customary cautious deliberation, 'He said somethang as to how he'd worked so damn hard on the round-up he was taking some rest and recreation and would be back in the marnin'. Seems like he an' Curly were headed into town.'

'Goddam him. I've told him to stay clear of Washoe City. And Curly's just a kid. He won't be much use if they run into Vincent and his men.'

'Waal, you've done all you can for that boy since he turned up outa the blue. You've tried mother-henning him but it don't work,' Dave crooned, as he stood hands on hips. 'Jeb's got a mind of his own. If you don't mind me saying, I sometimes think he's a tad loco.'

Matt glanced at him and sighed. 'You said it, Dave.

Seems to be he's taken after that drunken Irish galoot of a father of his. He's sure got wildness in his blood. But then so did I when I was his age.'

'He gets mighty hard-nosed if you ride him.'

'He sure does.'

'He's certainly developed a taste for whiskey and them wimmin at Gus's saloon, that's for sure.'

'The trouble is,' Matt said, pulling out his Peacemaker and checking the cylinder, 'since he shot that hard-arse Mason down and supposedly saved my life, he seems to think he's the fastest gun north of the Yellowstone. That, with his hair-trigger temper ain't a good combination.'

'Aw, ain't no use worryin', Matt. You've warned him. What more can you do? Anyhow, it ain't the end-of-the-month payday so the Tarantula boys ain't likely to be in town.'

'Guess so, but I don't like it. If he isn't back by the morning I'll have to go roust him out. I've ordered some pills mail order from Chicago. S'posed to cure lump jaw in cattle. I wanna call at the post office to see if they've arrived yet.'

As they wandered off to the corral Dave said, 'Have you seen any sign of it in our herd?'

'No,' Matt replied, 'but when one critter gets the disease it can spread across the pasture and infect others. I believe in being prepared.'

'Pills won't work,' Dave opined. 'The only remedy if they get it is to shoot 'em.'

'Thar they are. The goddamn rustlers.' Harriet peered from behind some rocks on a hilltop. 'I've got 'em.' She had the Long Tom propped on a rock aimed in their direction and adjusted the sights. 'I'd say they're 'bout a three-quarter mile away. I'll blow their durn heads off.'

But what if she missed? 'They might git away. No, I'll follow 'em.' She scrambled on to the skewbald, eased him down the hillside and set off across the plain in the direction that the two riders and stolen stock were headed. 'Maybe I should go git help?' she mused as she rode. 'No, I can handle 'em. This'll show Pa, Grat an' the boys I'm as good as any of 'em, if not better.

But when she rounded a finger of the hills she found they had disappeared. 'Where'n hell they gawn?' Harriet circled the skewbald back and found cloven-footed and iron-shod hoof-prints headed into the narrow Wild Cat Canyon. She jammed her floppy-brimmed hat down over her brow and followed the tracks at a cautious trot until they wheeled up into a coulée shielded by dense brush of mostly dead or dying alders. The girl slid to the ground, hitched the horse to a shrub and bent down, toting the heavy buffalo gun. She probed forward up the loose-earthed coulée, careful not to crack any dead branches. Pretty soon she heard the sound of voices.

Peeping through the foliage she saw the heifers backed up into a corner under a cliff and two punchers knelt feeding a fire with knots of wood. 'That red hair's a dead giveaway,' she whispered to herself, as she rested the Long Tom's barrel on a branch to take aim. 'And dead is what he's going to be. Prepare to meet Satan, pal.'

Boom! The big fifty calibre bullet whistled out with the screech of a banshee, smashing into the fire and sending the running iron hurtling. 'Damn!' Harriet cursed to grope for another bullet in her coat pocket. 'Missed!'

Fumbling, all fingers and thumbs, she managed to get another slug in the spout, but when she looked up the punchers had dived for cover. Where were they? Ah, yes, she could see frightened eyes beneath a curly mop peering over a rock. 'Come on out, you crab-louse,' she hollered in the deepest voice possible. 'That was just a warnin'. Grab air, 'cause next time I'm aimin' to kill. We got ya surrounded. Ain't no way you gonna wriggle out.'

Curly stepped out, hands in the air, crying, 'Don't shoot.'

'Toss your gun away and step forward,' she growled. 'Where's t'other one? Tell the li'l red-headed rat to show hisself, or else. . . . *Ouf!*'

The air was squashed from Harriet as Jeb landed on her back, flattening her face forward on the ground. She had lost her grip on the rifle and the cold barrel of his Sidewinder was pressed against her temple.

'You looking fer me, sweetheart?' Jeb giggled, gripping her by the neck, shoving her nose into the mossy earth. 'If it ain't Horrible Harriet. It's OK, Curly. What you scared of? It's only a gal. Or is she? Maybe she's a boy? Beats me.'

'I shoulda kilt you with that first shot, you filthy thievin' dingbat!' Harriet spluttered, as she twisted her head to scowl at them. 'Git orf me.'

'It's Harriet Vincent,' Curly said with awe.

'You don't say? Harriet the Lariat. The one who rides around pretending to be Bufflo Bill sceerin' us poor boys to death.'

'Hadn't we better let her go?'

'You jokin'? She knows too much now. Go get a rope.'

When he returned Curly jumped up into an alder to look over the bushes down to the plain. 'Ain't no sign of nobody.'

'That was just a bluff. Keep your gun on her while I. . . .' Jeb slipped the rawhide noose over her head, jerking it tight around her throat. He twisted her arms behind her and bound her wrists. 'Got her. All ready for branding.'

They dragged her towards the fire and dumped her unceremoniously on the ground. 'What you gonna do with her?' Curly asked, nervously.

'Dead men tell no tales. Nor do dead gals. Doncha

see, boy? We can't let her go now.'

'I don't like it. No man wants to be branded a woman-killer.'

'Don't make no odds to me, man or woman.' Jeb jabbed her with his boot. 'You are a woman, aincha, underneath them clothes?'

'You pickled pig's head,' she retorted, spread-eagled on her back. 'I caught ya red-handed, didn't I? You're the one behind the fence-cuttin' and rustlin'. T'other smelly polecat's just your stooge. Is Matthew Saunders in with you?'

'Matt? Nah. He's too much of a sceered old lady. He's lost his nerve.' Jeb straddled her again, gripping her between his knees, scratching at a red rash of acne on his thin face. 'I'm the one in charge.'

'Take me to him. I demand you do that. Matthew will know what to do with me. Doncha see? I'm much more valuable alive than dead to you. You can use me to bargain with.'

Jeb met her frank blues beneath her fringe and giggled. 'Pah! Matt would just send you home with a flea in your ear.' He bent down and licked at her lips. 'I got other plans for you, honey.'

'Euch! Git your spotty mug away from me,' Harriet spat in his face. 'I don't wanna catch your pox, you dirty ginger dwarf.'

'Right, you don't wanna do it the nice way,' Jeb shouted. 'Let's see what you got here.' Angrily he ripped her shirt apart, almost drooling over her as he

64

released her lily-white, pink-tipped breasts. 'Look at these, Curly. Real cute and tender. I do believe she ain't had a man lickin' at her afore.'

Helpless in her bonds, Harriet screamed, 'You dare to touch me. My daddy will kill you. Both of you. He'll hang you high.'

'He might just be a bit late.' Jeb jerked off her bandanna and tied it tight around her mouth. 'That'll shut her up. Cain't stand a woman screamin'. Never could. Get her boots off, Curly, and her chaps and pants.

Harriet wriggled and kicked furiously, but Curly hung on to her legs and did what he was bid. His reservations gone, the glimpse of her pale breasts had put fire in his loins, possessing his mind, turning him, too, into a maddened dog.

'Ride her, cowboy,' he hollered.

'Yay-hoo!' Jeb yodelled, turning to grope a filthy hand between her legs.

Harriet's eyes bulged as she strained against the gag, kicking and groaning. But she knew she was trapped.

EIGHT

Huge castles of silver-tinged clouds had built up in the blue skies, giving an even greater sensation of space to the wide, high country. Not so far off, the snowy peaks of the Rocky barrier loomed with a crystal-clear clarity in the sharp air.

'I wanna do a bit of hunting, Dave, think things over, decide what I'm gonna do. I'm gonna cinch up and light out on my own,' Matt told the old hand. 'I should be back by sundown.'

Dozy Dave knew what the ranch boss had to decide: whether to take a stand against Vincent. In other words, range war. Or maybe herd the stock into Miles City, get what he could for them in their scrawny, winter condition, cut his losses and pull out.

A fight, he knew, was likely to be a bloodbath in Vincent's favour, but he drawled, 'You know I'm behind you, Matt, an' I'm purty sure most of the boys are, too.'

'I employed y'all as cowhands not gunfighters, but we'll see. I guess I shoulda gone after Jeb, but I'm sick of nursemaiding that boy. It's too late now. He'll have to fight his own battles.'

'Aw, I wouldn't worry about him. He'll be in Gus's saloon sousing his brains with rotgut, and busier than a bunny in spring chasing them gals.'

'Yeah, I 'spect so.' Matt swung on to Crackers, and with a pony in tow as pack horse, headed out of the ranch. 'So long. See ya.'

It was good to get away from troubling thoughts of the crazy Joshua Vincent, barbed wire and his rebellious half-brother. He forded the snow-melt swollen river and rode on towards a region of dense thickets of diamond willow and buffalo berry fringing the foothills of the mountains.

Straight-backed, Matt rode deep in the saddle, his .40-.75 single-shot Sharps-Borchardt rifle stuck in the saddle cinch. Crackers seemed as glad as he to be out and about, eagerly manoeuvring through the rocky terrain.

After two hours' riding he spotted a herd of Big Horn mountain sheep up on a hill within easy gunshot. But the ram looked Matt square in the eye, gave the hike signal and they scooted away as fast as they could run.

Saunders had hesitated because he had seen a trickle of smoke rising from some trees not far off and he didn't want to give his presence away. Getting closer he spied the tops of buffalo-hide lodges poking through the treetops. A chill went up the hunter's spine: any man would know fear encountering Indians out here in the wilderness. It engendered caution. 'Who we got here?' he wondered, for he couldn't be sure if this might be one of the small tribe of hostiles that still roamed the land.

There was no point in trying to circumnavigate the encampment. He loosened the buckle of his Peacemaker's leather holster, thumbing it to full cock. A six-gun would be more use than the single-shot if it came to trouble. Then he rode forward and into the circle of tipis for he knew Indians respected a man who showed no outward sign of fear, even if he was tensed up inside.

Dogs barked, boys shouted warnings and women at their tasks drew their children into safety. A sturdy old warrior in fringed leggings, a red shirt and beaded moccasins, stepped from a lodge, his dark face impassive, making no sign of welcome.

Matt recognized Spotted Eagle, a Cheyenne chief who until recently had been one of the most implacable foes of the white man and perhaps still was. A dozen dark-skinned warriors, all with feathers entwined into top-knots of hair, holding spears and bows, had gathered malevolently about him.

The rancher raised his hand in the peace sign, wondering uncomfortably if they might have returned to their old habits. These were a different kettle of fish to the tame Indians who hung around the forts.

'Howdy,' he said, lamely. 'I'm just passing through.'

They were obviously suspicious of white men's treachery, but after an awkward few moments Spotted Eagle raised his hand, too, and asked him to step down and smoke with them.

Matt found a small sack of tobacco in his pack, and a few bright gewgaws, bracelets and beads for the women and children he carried as a kind of insurance for just such an occasion. He offered the baccy to the chief, who mixed it with his own willow bark, and filled his long pipe as he and his warriors sat cross-legged around their fire.

'We are tired of running from the long knives,' Spotted Eagle explained in sign language. 'We have laid down our weapons. We take no more hair.'

His warriors grinned at his scalping sign as if relishing the memories of their old raids. His two wives, in high-necked, decorative collars and blanket shawls, had come to sit behind him. 'They are sisters,' the chief explained. 'Sisters don't argue as much as other squaws.'

Matt took a drag of the acrid smoke and, trying not to choke, agreed. 'That sounds like a good idea.'

The whites had corrupted these people with whiskey, shot them down like animals, wiped out whole villages with diseases like smallpox, so 30,000

Cheyenne and Sioux had united in a frenzy to defend their lands. But they could not fight the overwhelming numbers and the army's howitzers, brave as they might be. It was a matter now of the last few bands fighting on to the death or bowing to the inevitable, as Spotted Eagle had.

There was good hunting in the breaks to the north they told him, and he wished them well and headed on his way. After another two hours' riding their words proved true. Through the bushes he suddenly saw the biggest bull elk he had ever encountered. What's more the short-sighted elk was upwind.

The rancher couldn't resist; he whispered to Crackers to hold still and slid the rifle out of the cinch. With its huge spread of antlers the elk was as big as his own horse. The bullet hit him behind the shoulder, a heart shot. The elk staggered, stumbled for fifty paces and collapsed; the Sharps and a master gunsmith had proved their two hundred dollars' worth. The rancher hurriedly finished the elk, slitting his throat.

How'n hell am I going to get him back? he wondered, for he could hardly move the dead beast who he guessed weighed more than five hundred pounds. I think I've bit off more'n I can chew here.

A whinny from Crackers alerted him, however, and looking up he saw a line of wild-looking riders coming over the hill. In big sombreros, bandoliers of bullets wound over their shoulders, brandishing lances and rifles, they gave shrill Spanish yips as they charged towards him driving a bunch of wild mustangs.

'Comancheros!' Matt exclaimed, grabbing his rifle to defend himself. For centuries such men had traded guns with the Indians in return for captured white women they took south of the border to sell to brothel hells. He took hasty aim and fired a warning shot over their heads. 'Jasus!' he muttered grimly. 'A single-shot against this bloodthirsty mob ain't gonna stop 'em. What they doing so far north?'

NINE

On they came, this gang of unruly *muchachos*, cracking whips, hollering in shrill Spanish, driving the herd of wild mustangs. A stallion was in the lead of his harem of mares, followed by their frightened foals galloping on in spite of his rifle shot. They came pounding towards him as he hurriedly reloaded, and it was then he saw there was a handful of Americans in their midst. Among them was a hairy, long-bearded man in greasy buckskins Matt recognized. A man with deformed lips and a gargantuan forehead. You couldn't mistake him: 'Mustang Ben!'

The young rancher put up his rifle as the *vaqueros* came charging in, circling and halting the mob of eye-rolling horses, holding them steady with long lances and cracking whips until some had jumped down to drag broken branches to corral them in against the big fallen tree where Matt stood with his elk.

'You put a scare in me, you old rogue,' Matt shouted over the din as Ben leapt from his powerful quarter horse to land lightly on moccasined feet and stuck out his broad hand. 'I thought you were Comancheros invading our land.'

'Nah.' Ben twisted his puffed-up lips in what passed for a grin. 'Them days is over, *amigo*. How ya doin', Matthew? Fancy bumpin' into you agin.'

He slapped and mock-punched the rancher, hugging him. 'Been doin' a bit of hunting? This elk's a beauty, ain't he?'

'Biggest I've ever seen. I was just thinking I'd have to abandon part of him for the wolves.'

'Aw, don't worry, my wolves are hungry enough to eat a dozen of him.' Mustang Ben snapped out orders in rapid Spanish. His *ciboleros* swung down from their silver-decorated, high-pommelled saddles and began swiftly gutting and butchering the beast. As the stallion in his brush corral reared and whinnied his anger, they soon had a pine wood fire blazing and sat around roasting strips of meat, dangling it from greenwood sticks over the fire like the Indians did.

'I prefer mine roasted in the ashes,' Matt said, poking a couple of thick tenderloin steaks into the glowing embers as the flames died down. 'How about you, Ben?'

'Yah, sure, gits nice an' crumpy that way.'

He was one of the old frontiersmen. He had

driven a stage cross-country from St Louis to Los Angeles, chased by Indians most of the way, before the Central Pacific railroad put an end to that. He had panned for gold as a young man in the California rush, travelled the length and breadth of the old West, fought in the Mexican war and sought silver in the mines at Durango. But mostly now he made his living as a wrangler, capturing and breaking wild mustangs for sale.

'The herds are getting scarce on the southern plains,' he said. 'That's why we've come north.'

His companions were a hard-looking bunch, their faces tanned like saddle leather; among them were three Americans Matt vaguely recognized, a gangly backwoodsman, One Eye Jack, the black-bearded Whiskey-guts Ryan, who had ridden with Jesse James and a notorious Texan bank robber, Halo Waters, not men he would care to cross.

'Musta been in Denver in '76 I last saw Matt,' Ben yelled to them. 'He saved my bacon that day in a little saloon fracas.'

'Aw,' Matt grinned. 'I don't like to see a good man put down.'

He found it difficult not to stare at Ben's huge lips and red-hued gargoyle face amid all the hair. He had never asked him the cause of his ugliness but heard it had been a drunken doctor twisting his head in his forceps at his birth. Matt's father had taught him to read but had only one book, *The Hunchback of Notre*

74

Dame, and Ben had always reminded him of Quasimodo. Like Ben old Quasi might have been ugly, but he had a heart of gold.

'So, whatcha doin' out here in these lonesome breaks on your ownsome?' Ben asked. 'The posse after ya, or somethang?'

'No, nuthin' so easy. I got a small ranch thirty miles off over yonder,' Matt waved vaguely. 'Employ eight hands, along with my troublesome half-brother.'

'A rancher, huh? You've sure gone up in the world.'

'I decided it was time to put down roots, try to make something of myself. But ranching ain't all honey, believe me.'

'We was gonna run these hosses into Billings, or on to Miles City, but, I'll tell you what, Matt, you can have 'em for half-price. We'll break 'em for ya, too.'

'No.' Matt shook his head. 'We could certainly do with some more horses for the remuda, but I ain't got any spare cash at the moment.'

'Aw, you can owe it me. You'll be taking your herd into market in September, won't ya? You can pay me then or give me one of them bank cheques I can cash later in the year. You'll be in the money then, woncha?'

'It ain't so easy, Ben. I got troubles. I ain't sure I'll still be around these parts in September.'

'Troubles?' Ben chewed on his succulent steak,

blood trickling into his beard with every bite. 'You mean troubles of the gunfightin' sort?'

'It's not your problem, Ben. I can handle it. If not, I'm just gonna have to back off.'

'Your problem is my problem, pal. I ain't jokin'. Anythang me and the boys can do to help, we will. I owe ya.'

'You don't owe me nuthin', Ben. But,' Matt said, with a sigh, 'if you really want to know there's two of us ranching that valley, one crazy ol' 'coon who's been there years and me, a smaller outfit up the north end. You heard of Joshua Vincent? He's trying to push me out. In fact, he sent three guys to kill me last week. As you see, they didn't succeed.'

'That don't sound fair,' Ben mused. 'You mean he's got a bigger outfit than yourn?'

'Yep, he outnumbers me two-to-one. We been growling at each other like a couple of bobcats with one tree between 'em for years, but it's suddenly got serious. To top it all I got this half-wit half-brother who seems intent on making matters worse.'

Mustang Ben chewed at his meat some more, gripping it in his hands, silent for some time. 'If this fella Vincent's bringing in fast guns. . . .' he wiped his greasy hands on his leggings. 'Funny, ain't it? Seems like we just turned up in time.'

'It's not your battle, Ben. You go on your way.'

'No way, pardner.' Ben sprang to his feet and rattled out Spanish at the Mexican *ciboleros*, who gave flashing smiles and yells, brandishing the lances they used to control bulls and kill buffaloes from horse-back. 'Yeah, they all agree. Your battle is our battle.'

'I can't afford—'

'You just hire us as punchers at your usual rate, what is it, twenty-a-month all found? Put our wages on the bill come meat-packing time when you're sittin' on McQueen's veranda among the other rich ranchers. No arguin', Matthew. Come on. Where is this ranch of yourn? Let's go, *muchachos*.'

'OK, you're on the payroll.' Matt offered his hand again to seal the deal. 'But don't say I didn't warn you. There's trouble brewing.'

'Hey, git in your saddle, Halo,' Whiskey-guts hollered. 'I smell gunfightin' weather.'

Roped hand and foot, sore in body and mind, Harriet lay on the filthy mud floor of her prison. It was one of those dug-outs wolfers used, barely visible if out on the plains, but almost invisible up here in the coulée. A dark, smelly hole at the base of the cliff with the stink of rotten animal guts and strychnine. In fact a big brown bottle of the stuff stood in a corner ominously marked 'Poison'. The wolfers soaked a ball of tallow in it and left it for their prey. They were paid a bounty by the state, or cattlemen, on the pelts. They even sold the poor critters' furs to furriers. Whoever had lived here had long since deserted it.

77

After the rapes, as she curled up in a corner, shuddering, sore and sobbing, they had let her have her pants back, tidy herself up. 'Quit that damn wailing,' Jeb had warned, 'or we'll have to gag you again.' Curly had given her a mug of black coffee, and they had gone back to branding the stolen stock. Free of her bonds, Harriet had waited her chance and made a wild dash for liberty. Halfway down the coulée she had tripped on a tree root and Jeb had landed on her back again. 'Doncha try that,' he had screamed, giving her vicious slaps across the face. 'We tryin' to be nice to you.' He noosed her and dragged her, torn and bleeding, back to the dug-out.

'What you so worried about?' he jeered, tossing her a bit of beef jerky as if she was a dog. 'We all gotta die some day.'

'Balanced on that sharp edge twixt life and death,' Curly quoted, melodramatically, 'as Matthew said when we buried old Len.'

Before leaving they had trussed her like a chicken, gagged her again, said they would be back sometime and herded off the stock. Harriet thought of Matthew's words. They weren't exactly comforting.

TEN

Washoe City had come into being five years before when a seam of gold had been discovered up in the hills and another stampede was on. But the rush didn't last long; the seam fizzled out. A handful of prospectors had remained, poking with their picks around the played-out mines, but they barely found enough dust to pay for their groceries and whiskey each week. Other folk, who had arrived to service their needs, a blacksmith's livery, Chinese laundry, gunshop, barber's and bathhouse, meat market, saloons, restaurants and so forth, found their profits neglible. Most of them, the gamblers and goodtime girls, packed up and moved on looking for the next big rush.

But a staunch few had remained, catering mainly for the needs of the outlying ranches. The population had dwindled to three hundred or so, Washoe City no longer had a lot to recommend it; there was no telegraph line, school, doctor, railroad or stage service. Most of the dwellings were of log or of whip-sawed cottonwood boards. Goods were hauled in by a six-horse freighter once a month, except in winter when below-zero temperatures meant snow often blocked the pass. The summers were fiercely hot. Even in May, though, there could be lightning storms and hail. The only good point was that the Indian tribes had been subdued. A few years before they had terrorized most of the Yellowstone valley. Now, with any luck, a citizen could ride into Billings without losing his or her hair.

'Something's got to be done,' the portly Horace Poulson, in his frock coat and black silk plug hat, shouted, hammering his fist for order at the crowded town meeting in Gus's saloon. 'We can't have Joshua Vincent dictating to us who we can sell goods to or even talk to. The ranchers are at each others' throats. Three men were killed on this very spot only days ago. Washoe City needs some law and order.'

'Hear! Hear!' Gus Brown roared, propping up his own bar. 'Look what Vincent did to my eye when I complained about his thugs coming in here. It's time we appointed a sheriff afore any more of us get hurt.'

'Who'n tarnation's gonna take that durn job?' Mrs McGinty, the boarding house keeper, screeched. 'We need to send to Fort Benton and git an army patrol down here.'

'Aw, they ain't int'rested in us,' Poulson moaned.

80

'I've tried. They're too busy rounding up the hostiles. I propose we form a town committee. I'm prepared to stand as mayor and push our demands with the territorial authorities. We need protection.'

'What'n hell will *they* do?' the blacksmith, Eph Smith, scoffed, ' 'cept send a tax-collector?'

'So, what other suggestions do you have?' Poulson demanded, wiping a drip from his bulbous, purple-veined nose. 'Any sensible comments?'

'Yeah!' Harold Hawkins got up from his chair by the fire, waving a tankard. 'I want another whiskey.'

'Whiskey will be available at my special offer price of forty cents a glass at the end of the meeting, so sit down and shut up,' Gus Brown bellowed, amid laughter.

'This is a life or death matter. Vincent threatened to burn me down. And the rest of the town,' Gus shouted. 'My chimney breast is made of bricks specially imported at seventy-five cents a brick. It serves its purpose but not if there's an arsonist around.'

'Nobody likes Vincent's threats,' the barber, Samuel Katzenjammer, whined. 'He told me I mustn't trim the hair of Longbranch men. What can we do? I am no gunman. Do you know people avoid Washoe City because of our violent reputation?'

'The only thing that can be done is for every member of our business community to pay a weekly rate for the salary of a lawman,' Poulson cried. 'We need a strong, independent-minded man, who's not afraid to use a gun. The first move is to place an advertisement in the *Yellowstone Journal* for such a man.'

'You won't git nobody under a hundred dollars a month,' Gus remarked, morosely.

'So,' Poulson replied, 'we will have to raise that on a regular basis. Isn't our safety worth a dollar a week from each of us?'

'Har! Har! Har!' Croaking, sarcastic, mock laughter from behind them made the audience jump, almost like naughty children, because they knew who it was even before they owled their heads to look at Joshua Vincent.

He was leaning over the batwing doors. How long had he been listening? How much had he heard?

'You lousy traitors!' He shouted with undisguised contempt as he pushed inside. 'Plotting your devious schemes behind my back, are ya? You know what they do with turncoats? Shoot 'em!'

'Sir!' Poulson leaned his fists on his table, rising to meet the old patriarch as he stomped down the aisle. 'We citizens have every right to discuss our protection without being subjected to threats by you.' His rosy face displayed his dismay as Grat and a dozen gun-toting ranch-hands clattered inside and lined up along the back. 'Or your thugs.'

'Thugs?' Joshua's craggy face, his long, white hair dangling around it beneath his black hat, was irate. He poked a finger at Poulson's protuberant nose.

'You jumped up blowfly, that's all y'are, sucking blood out of these people here with your cheatin' prices for your inferior stuff.'

'How dare you, sir!' Mrs Poulson jumped up to defend her spouse. 'All we take is an honest profit. Our aim in calling this meeting is to help these people.'

'Ye're both a coupla thievin' packrats,' Joshua shouted. 'It's time you were tarred and feathered and run outa town. So shut up.'

'That not polite. No talk to lady like that,' Wang Hu, of the Chinese laundry, chipped in. 'We need proper sheriff this town. Not you.'

'What?' Vincent spun round, grabbed him by his shirt front and held him dangling. 'You jumped up li'l slitty-eyes. Go back to Chink-land if you don't like it here.' He hurled him away, calling back to Grat, 'Put him on the list.'

'Vot you do, Mr Vincent?' demanded Katzen-jammer, the barber, or 'capillary manipulator', as he described himself. 'You going to shoot us all? We live in modern times. We got right be here. People of many nations come here. We believe this Land of Free.'

'What? Now a damn Hun's telling me what I gotta do? Listen, you croakers and milksops, it's because of men like me that you are free, yeah, so you can sleep in your beds all safe and sound. Where were you when we carved out this country? Where were you when for twenty years or more we did battle day and night with the ceaseless raids of them screaming savages? Whoja think made this land nice an' cozy so lice like you could crawl in and think you could take over without risking your cowardly hides? You scum make me sick. I've given you my ultimatum: you cross the line again it will be another war – you aginst me.'

'Those days are over, Joshua,' Gus Brown summoned the nerve to interject. 'You're living in the past. Mr Katzenjammer's right. We gotta catch up with the rest of the world. Even General Crook says so. Look!' He waved a copy of the *Yellowstone Journal.* 'It says he entertained Dull Knife and his three daughters at dinner in the officers' mess at Fort Robinson t'other day.'

'*What?*' Joshua screeched, his coat tails flying as he dragged out his revolver and spun around as if under attack from all sides, carooming shots smashing into the woodwork, one whipping off Poulson's black silk plug hat, as his men joined in and the audience screamed and struggled to escape. When the explosions racketed to an end, Vincent stood, his pistol smoking, panting like a pursued wolf in the emptied room. 'That butcher Dull Knife,' he croaked. 'That looney Crook, the Injin-lover. Yeck! What's this country coming to?'

'You can come out from behind them barrels, Gus,' Grat shouted. 'Pour the whiskies. You sure got my daddy roostered up!'

The barkeep got to his feet and reached for a bottle. 'All General Crook was saying is we gotta forget old hatreds, forge a new society—'

'Yeah,' the ramrodder, Dusty, snarled. 'Mr Vincent don't agree with all that crap. Neither do we.'

ELEVEN

'What's all the commotion?' Jeb wondered, as they heard the sound of gunfire rolling across the prairie from the direction of Washoe City.

'Beats me,' Curly replied, as they herded the heifers along. But by the time they reached town, Joshua Vincent and his men had left and all was quiet again.

They got a reasonable price from Sam for the beeves, no questions asked, and got stuck into beef-burgers and coffees in Milly Mackay's restaurant. She also provided Jeb with paper and pencil at his request and, with much grunting and head-scratching he composed their letter. 'Howja spell first?' he asked. 'Yah, thass right.'

Jeb had never excelled academically at his village school. He was more proficient at gouging, shouting, kicking, tugging girls' pigtails and similar anti-social behaviour in the playground. But he was quite proud of the laboured result:

'We hav got yore doorter. Cum to Wild Kat canyun at sunup. Alone. Furst lite of dorn. Bring $5,000. Then yu hav her bak. If yu ar not alone she dyes.'

He put it in an envelope, licking the seal, gave the maid, Titty Tess, as they called her, a cartwheel dollar and told her to take it over the road to the post office, which was one service Washoe City *did* have. The mailman and his cart would deliver the letter the next day out at Vincent's ranch.

'What do we do,' Curly asked, 'when we've got all that money?'

'We kill him,' Jeb replied, drily. 'And her. Then git the hell outa Washoe County. We'll head for Virginny City.'

'Do we *have* to kill her?' Curly demurred. 'I don't like—'

'Of course we do. Nobody knows it's us. That's the way it's got to stay,' he hissed, getting to his feet and tossing another dollar to Tess. 'C'mon, boy. Let's go lubricate our tonsils along at Gus's. We're gonnabe rich.'

'I ain't supposed to serve you,' the big barkeep complained. 'Look how Vincent and his boys roughed up my saloon. It was sheer luck nobody got killed.'

'He sure made them shopkeepers run,' Harold Hawkins cackled from his chair by the fire.

'Aw, come on, Gus,' Jeb coaxed. 'We're in the

money.' He rolled a couple of silver dollars along the counter to Gus. 'And, look, just to show I got no hard feelin's I brought you a big fat cigar.'

Surprised, Gus mumbled his thanks, filled them tumblers of Knock 'Em Dead, his own mixture, and put the cigar to one side.

The clink of cartwheels was like a magnet to the girls in the backroom. Alice and two other sisters of sin quickly cosied up around Jeb and Curly as they bought drinks for all in the bar. 'Aincha gonna give us some of your lovin'?' Alice murmured, her fingers dipping enticingly into Jeb's trousers.

'Aw, I'm a bit fagged out today,' Jeb muttered. 'We've had a busy time.'

'Yeah,' Curly giggled, nudging him. 'Why pay fer it when we can get it fer free?'

'What you talking about?' Alice asked. 'You got another sweetheart someplace?' She dibbled her tongue in his ear, cooing, 'She couldn't give you such a nice time as me.'

'Aw, I dunno,' Jeb grinned, pushing her away. 'Nuthin' like fresh meat. Hey, Gus, aincha gonna smoke that fine cigar?' He winked at the girls. 'Watch this.'

'Yeah,' Curly sniggered. 'Then we better git back to see our ladyfriend. She cain't get enough of us.'

'You bastards,' Alice screamed, as Gus lit his cigar which, stuffed with gunpowder, exploded in his face.

Jeb snatched up the bottle, grabbed Curly and

shouted, 'See y'all.' They ran outside, laughing and shouting, jumped on their mustangs and headed back to Wild Cat canyon. It was time to have some more fun.

'Why me?' Gus moaned, his face blackened by gunpowder, his shirt ripped, his hands shaking as he spat out the remains of the cigar. 'What have *I* done?'

'That measly little pock-faced rat.' Alice scowled, and suddenly burst into tears. 'He said he loved me.'

'What's the matter with you?' Gus said. 'You losin' your touch? You shoulda creamed all them dollars outa him.'

'I tried,' Alice sniffled. 'But he wasn't in the mood.'

'That's strange. There's somethun' funny going on,' Gus pondered. 'What are them two up to?'

When Harriet didn't return by noon from her morning gallop out on the range, Polly began to get anxious about her. 'Where do you think she's got to?' she asked her Aunt Martha.

'Aw, you ain't no need to worry about Harriet. She'll be out prowling around the hills with that rifle of her'n looking fer them rustlers.'

'But what if she's run into them?'

'Aw, Harri will be OK,' her aunt said. 'She ain't like you eastern gals.'

Martha never lost the opportunity of rubbing that in and Polly was getting increasingly tired of her innuendoes that any woman born east of Kansas was, among the other assertions, congenitally hopeless.

'Harri's probably heard about the town meeting and gone off to join her father and the boys to have a bit of fun.'

'A bit of fun,' Polly echoed. 'What do you mean?'

'Ain't nuthin' fer you to worry your head about. You got that chillied beef on the boil yet? It'll need a bit of stewing. If you have, go get me a side of bacon from the cold store.'

'Hasn't she ever heard of the word "please"?' Polly wondered, crossly, as she attempted to roll back boulders from pine planks protecting a big hole in the ground from hungry critters. This was the so-called cold store, lined bottom and sides with flat stones, which she eventually climbed down into. It served its purpose in the winter but in the summer, she imagined, was far from ideal. She found a bacon side and lugged it back to the kitchen, and so the day wore on with no sign of Harri, her uncle or the men.

The recent spring weather of exhilarating blue skies had vanished, and now grey mist rolled from the mountainsides and cloaked the range with sullen, louring clouds.

The shades of night were closing in when Harriet's skewbald suddenly came charging in at a high trot dragging an elder bush to which its reins were hitched, apparently torn from the ground by the impatient horse.

Polly ran to catch and soothe it, leading the skew-bald into the corral. 'She must have had an accident,' she called, as her aunt came running out to join her. 'I think I should go look for her or, at least warn Uncle Joshua.'

'*You*, what can *you* do?' her aunt screeched, con-temptuously, but it was obvious she, too, was worried by now. She watched Polly remove the saddle and sling it over the rail. 'You better wash him down first. It's gonna be a cold night. That hoss has come a long way, maybe twenty miles. He's all sweated-up; we don't want to lose him.'

Polly led him into the barn and, fretting at the delay, cried, 'Can't *you* do this? I'll take one of the other horses from the remuda.'

'Iffen you can catch one,' Martha scoffed. She pointed across the plain to some hills. 'You go across to Gunbarrel Canyon. Joshua said somethang about having some dehorning an' castratin' to do along there. If there ain't no sign of him you come straight back, you hear? It'll be pitch dark soon.'

'Right, I'll just get a couple of carrots from the kitchen,' the girl replied, running off. She was cer-tainly not adept with a lariat, so used the carrots to tempt a mustang to her. He was reasonably tame and she slipped the bridle over his head and the skew-bald's saddle on his back, cinching it tight. She led him out of the corral, climbed on the rail and jumped astraddle, going charging away she was not sure where.

The mustang certainly could run as Polly hung on to the reins and balanced on his back. Her boots in the bentwood stirrups, her skirts tucked up around her knees, her black hair streaming in the wind, she sat in the high-horned saddle and began to fall into the rhythm of the horse's stride, peering into the gloom. When they reached the far side of the plain she ventured up into a high-walled canyon, which must have been the one her aunt meant, but there was no sign or sound of Uncle Joshua or his men. Maybe there had been trouble in town. Something urged her to keep on going, skirting the side of the mountains in the semi-darkness. Maybe if Harriet had had a fall she would find her. When the moon suddenly climbed from behind a peak amid the fast-drifting clouds she could see more clearly as it glinted on the silver sage stretching across the seemingly limitless plain. It urged her to kick her heels into the mustang's sides to go faster; she charged on.

TWELVE

'You seen any sign of Polly?' Martha called as Joshua Vincent slammed the front door of the ranch house and stomped inside, putting his rifle away in the rack. 'She rode over to Gunbarrel Canyon to look for you.'

'Nope.' He glowered at his wife. 'What's the dratted girl up to? Why you let her go?'

'I couldn't stop her. She just saddled up and rode off. I told her to come back if she didn't find you. Is Harriet with ya?'

'Nope. Why should she be with us? We been into town, then as we were up that way did some work re-wiring. Somebody's pulled the fence down again and I've a hunch there's some cows missing. It's Saunders for sure. The sooner him and his brother are hanging high the happier I'll be. Why? Where *is* Harriet?'

'That's what I'm asking you. I'm worried, Josh. She

93

ain't been back since early this marnin'.'

'What?' the rancher thundered. 'And you've let the other one go looking fer her? That's two missing girls we got now.' Vincent grabbed his rifle again. 'Guess we gotta go look for 'em.'

'Have your dinner first. Y'all must be tired out. It's no use going out on an empty belly. The men gotta be fed too.'

'Yeah, I guess so.' Vincent tossed off his hat and went into the kitchen. 'They won't like being rousted out again. Seems to be nuthin' but trouble these days. What's Harriet playing at? And that other silly, stuck-up creature. It'll serve her right if she falls off and breaks her neck. It's a dark, blowy night; not much moon.'

'Oh, Josh,' Martha moaned, clutching at him for comfort. 'Don't say that. She's gone without a hat or coat, too. At least Harri knows how to look after herself.'

'Yeah? I ain't so sure about that. It's time that gal grew up,' he growled, as he sat down at the table and Martha sloshed beef stew into a bowl for him.

Trussed up on the floor of the dugout Harriet heard the sound of voices, horses whinnying and hoped desperately for seconds that it was her father, or even Matthew come to rescue her. But no, it was only them two.

'Her horse has gone,' Jeb said. 'This is bad. It'll

give 'em an idea where we are. We cain't afford to light a fire tonight. It might lead 'em to us if they're out lookin' for her.' He led the way down into the dugout, struck a match and lit a candle in a bottle, its glimmer illuminating the frightened girl. 'This is all we can chance using. Hello, darlin'. Bet you're pleased to see us back aincha?'

Harriet mumbled an oath through her gag. 'You promise to be nice an' we'll release you for a bit. OK?'

Jeb whipped away the gag and Harriet cried, 'Git these damn ropes offen me. I gotta go in the bushes. I can't wait.'

Jeb and Curly laughed at her discomfort and hurry, but led her out with just a rope around her throat.

'And don't you animals go peeping at me,' she yelled, as she rushed into the elders.

'Hurry it up, sweetheart,' Jeb called. 'We brought ya a bit of pie for your supper. Then we gonna have some more fun.'

'Aw, no,' Harriet groaned. 'Not *him*. Not *that* again. Gawd!'

Jeb went to unsaddle the horses and hitch them for the night as Curly hung on to her rope. When Harriet came out of the bushes she grabbed the younger cowboy's arm. 'I like you, Curly,' she whispered. 'You're OK. I ain't gonna say anythang aginst you when they rescue me.' Harriet nosed her head forward and pecked at his lips. 'You ain't gonna let him kill me, are you?'

'I dunno,' Curly muttered. 'Jeb's the one calls the shots. It depends on the cash.'

'Lordy, is that all that's worryin' you?' she whispered more intensely. 'You shoot that mad dog friend of yourn in the back my daddy will reward ya. Ten dollars, twenty dollars, I mean thousands. I promise you that. Then us two can git wed. I'll be a wealthy heiress when I come into my share of the ranch. We'll live happy ever after, have lots of kids.'

'Mm?' The cowboy considered this. 'Maybe you'd come into it sooner if I shot your daddy and Grat, too.'

'Sure,' she whispered, squeezing his hand and trying to kiss him again. 'Why not? I really like you. Shoot 'em all.'

'What's going on?' Jeb demanded, as he returned from the horses. 'What you two nattering about? What you up to?'

'Nuthin',' Curly stuttered. 'How about we have a slug of that whiskey you got?'

'Don't get any ideas, son.' Jeb jabbed the barrel of his Sidewinder into Curly's half-open mouth. 'You know you're no match for me. I'll splatter your brains all over these rocks you try anything.'

Curly gobbled like a turkey, his eyes bulging as Jeb thumbed back the hammer.

'Come on, you two morons,' Harriet growled.

'Where's that pie? I'm starving. You jest ain't got no idea how to treat a lady.'

'Aincha got no hooch, Matt?' Mustang Ben shouted, after he and his *ciboleros* had come roistering into the ranch that night driving the herd of wild mustangs before them. 'This is an occasion we oughta celebrate.'

'Yep.' One-Eye Jack hollered. 'Ahm as dry as a whore on a Sunday marnin'. Ain't wet my whistle fer nigh on two weeks.'

'No,' Matt replied. 'I don't allow drinking on the ranch so I ain't got none. Sorry, boys, you'll have to make do with coffee.'

'What's the matter with you, Matt?' Mustang Ben joshed him. 'You become a damn teetotal baptist or somethang?'

'My driftin' and drinkin' days are over,' Matt replied quietly.

They had all crammed into the small ranch house kitchen, stuffing themselves with sourdough biscuits.

'You boys still hungry?' the rancher asked.

'Nope, we told ya,' One-Eye put in. 'Thirsty's the word. C'mon, Mustang, let's head for the saloon.'

Matt wondered why the big, gangling backwoodsman, One-Eye, was so called for he seemed to have two eyes although one rolled around in an alarming manner. But in the West many men went by a pseudonym and it wasn't polite or wise to inquire about

97

their name or past.

'Washoe City's fifteen miles away,' Matt said. 'Ain't you boys had enough riding for one day?' He glanced at the kitchen clock. 'It's nine. I'd have thought you'd be tuckered out. My hands generally turn in about ten. If you join 'em over in the bunkhouse they'll dig up some extra blankets for you.'

'Just this one time, Matt.' Mustang Ben slapped him on the back, his gargoyle face splitting into a grin. 'I promised them. Nuthin's gonna hold 'em back. The lure of that saloon is like a magnet to them. We got plenty of fresh hosses. We'll be there in no time.'

'Yeah,' Whiskey-guts Ryan groaned. 'I need alcohol. It's like oxygen to me. Cain't live without it. We been up in them mountains too long.'

'Come on, you po-face.' Halo Waters stood behind Matt and mussed his hair over his eyes. 'Git ya glad rags on and come with us. I cain't wait to git my hands on one of them purty gals I been hearin' about.'

'I guess you win this time.' Matt grinned as he stood up and led them out into the yard. 'Let's go saddle up.'

The mild-mannered Dave looked bewildered by the arrival of the high-spirited mustang hunters. 'You sure it was a good idea putting these characters on the payroll?' he asked, amid the Mexicans' hollers of joy as they roped fresh mounts.

'They ain't gonna be here for long. Just until this trouble with Joshua Vincent blows over.'

'Hmm?' Dave scratched at his long jaw. 'Seems to me you already got one hellraiser here without taking on another handful.'

'You mean Jeb? Any sign of him?'

'Nope.'

'In that case maybe it's best I go take a look for him.'

Matt had to silently admit to himself, though, that he had misgivings about taking on Mustang Ben and his boys. 'They sure are a bunch of scarums,' he muttered, as with shrieks and yells they leapt on to their horses and set off at an urgent lope out into the night. 'I better go keep an eye on 'em.'

THIRTEEN

Polly was lost. She hung on to the reins of the strong-necked pony as it was spooked by the howl of a coyote echoing from a ravine. Or was it a coyote? She managed to haul the mustang around as another shriek pierced the night. An animal, prey to a preda-tor? Or could it be a female human's scream?

They had galloped across the plain, the girl rider both frightened and somehow elated by the pound-ing beast between her thighs, letting the horse have its head, carrying her on into the unknown. Then they had come up against the dark, craggy mass of the Crazy Mountains and swerved along its edge, passing numerous narrow, twisted arroyos which could surely only harbour snakes, prairie foxes or even wildcats among the undergrowth.

The scream split the night silence again as Polly pulled the horse to a halt. 'Oh, my God!' she whis-pered. 'Is that Harri?'

What to do? She was unarmed. Should she ride to get help? But she was no longer sure in which direction lay Washoe City or the Tarantula ranch. The half moon had risen high, casting an eerie glow across the landscape when it emerged from the silver-edged clouds. Polly slipped from the horse and led it up into the bushes of the ravine. Then she hitched the reins to a branch. Perhaps it would be wise to go on foot.

She crept through the tangled undergrowth on the loose, mossy ground towards the source of the screams and responding curses. Yes, that was Harri's twangy drawl. 'Get off me! No, please. Don't!' She sounded both indignant and frightened.

'You do what I tell ya,' a man's voice answered her. 'Or else! You want some more of the treatment?'

Now Polly was close enough to see a wiry young man kneeling on the half-naked, upturned girl, his hand raised, and the crack of leather on flesh as he belted her bare bottom. Her attacker gave a hysterical laugh as he flayed her. 'Howja like that, you stupid bitch?'

Polly licked her lips, torn between running for her own life, and attempting to save the girl. She looked around desperately for a small boulder she could use to hit him with on the back of his head – that would finish him.

But as Harriet howled, another youth, more a boy, emerged from some sort of hole in the ground. 'Jeb!'

101

he shouted, his own voice shrill. 'Leave her alone.'

Jeb froze, his belt upraised. 'What?' He turned, and in the moonlight Polly could see his acne-inflamed face was venomous. 'Did I hear right? Are *you* giving me orders?'

'It ain't right. She ain't doin' that. It ain't natural.'

'It's filthy!' Harri screamed. 'Shoot him,Curly.'

Polly, like Jeb, suddenly saw that the boy had a revolver in his hand. It was pointed at Jeb, who screamed an oath and made a dive at the boy, leaping at him like an attacking lynx. And like such a wildcat he twisted and howled as the bullet hit him mid-leap to send him sprawling in the dust.

For moments, in the semi-darkness, there was silence. All three stared at the slumped body. And Curly yelled, 'I kilt him. See! I done it.'

Polly ran from the bushes to put an arm around Harri, who was struggling to get up. 'It's all right,' she crooned, holding her. 'It's all over.'

'What? Where the hail did you come from?' Harriet demanded. 'Get orf me. I'm OK.'

'Who's she?' Curly demanded, turning his gun on Polly.

'Oh, my damn smarty-boots cousin from back east. Don't ask me how she got here. Where's my daddy?' she sniffled, wiping tears from her muddy, slap-reddened face. 'Pity it weren't *her* you two grabbed. You mighta had more fun.'

It was just a front, Polly knew, Harriet was shaking,

in a state of shock. She must have been through a terrible ordeal.

'You did the right thing, Curly, whoever you are,' Polly said. 'It was very brave of you. But put that gun away. We've got to get her home.'

'I dunno,' Curly stammered. 'That might not be a good idea. Mr Vincent ain't gonna like this. I think we'd better head into town where I got some protection. Kinda sort things out there.'

'Well, I rely on you to lead us. I'm lost.'

'Yeah, *you* would be,' Harriet groaned, as she found her pants and pulled them on. 'How'd you find us anyhow?'

'Purely by chance. I heard your screams.'

'Screams? *I* ain't a screamer. Don't you go telling that to folks.'

'Come on, Harri.' Polly helped her on with her coat. 'You'll feel better when we get to town. Do you think you can ride?'

'Yeah.' Harriet clutched at Polly and tears trickled down her cheeks. 'I think so. I'm hurtin' real bad.'

Polly comforted her and when she was calmer they helped her on to Jeb's horse. Curly glanced at the prone body of Jeb and led them back down the ravine. Polly jumped on her own mustang and they headed away across the plain.

FOURTEEN

Of the three calico queens at the Washoe City Saloon the young and comely Alice, well decked with a cheeky grin whatever the weather, usually reigned supreme. But on this cacophonous night her unashamedly obese friend, the barrel-bellied Daisy, was giving her a run for her money.

'Your Latinos seem addicted to the larger lady,' Matt remarked, as he stood at the bar, a bottle of steam beer in his hand.

'Yeah,' Mustang Ben agreed, as Daisy, her vast posterior barely covered by a frilly, girlie dress of polka-dot design, wobbled once more towards the back room, escorted by two *ciboleros* fighting to be first in possession. 'No accounting for taste. Guess they want as much as they can git for their cash.'

'Mm,' Matt reflected. 'So many cents a pound.'

He had questioned Gus and the girls about Jeb and the fact that his visit that day had been brief bothered him. He had been and gone. Like the 'keep said, something funny was going on. But where? And what?

'Me,' Ben was reflecting, 'I prefer the skinny old dame. Why don't you give her a try, Matt? Goes like a rattlesnake.'

'No thanks,' Matt declined with a grin, for Leonara, the lady in question, whose delights Mustang Ben had been the first to sample, was tottering from the back room in tight high-heeled boots, her varicose-veined legs encased in crumpled stockings gartered above her knobbly knees. The rest of her emaciated body was adorned in a silky, scarlet *peignoir*, trimmed with tatty fur, from which one lumpy, listless breast had escaped.

'Whoo!' Leonara exclaimed. 'Them Mex galoots certainly put a gal through the mangle. I'm fair fagged out.'

'Here,' Matt said, 'take a pew,' and helped her aboard a wooden stool between them. 'Take a breather. Sounds like you've earned it.'

'Thank you, kind sir. Feel quite whoozy.' Leonara vaguely waved gnarled fingers about her pouchy face. All the flour paste she had plastered on, the red paint on her wrinkly lips, could not disguise her age. 'Sometimes I think I'm gettin' past it for this game.'

'Nonsense,' Ben roared. 'You're the best.'

'Yes, handsome here' – she patted the gorgon-faced backwoodsman on his hairy head – 'wasn't backward in coming forward.'

'No time to hang about,' Gus Brown warned her, as he raked in more silver dollars. 'We ain't gonna have a night like this again for a while.'

'Yes, more's the pity.' Leonara bared her toothless gums in a leer. 'I'm just engaging these gentlemen in genteel conversation.'

'Sure.' Mustang slapped another dollar down. 'Same again, Mr Brown, and one for the lady.'

When the visitors were finally sated they settled down to gambling, reminiscing or whirling Alice in her flared dress around the floor of the barnlike saloon as an old gent in a battered top hat and worn frock coat sat at a small harmonium pumping out discordant melodies.

Daisy, in her frilly dress, had staggered from the backroom, collapsed on to a groaning horsehair sofa and refused to budge again.

Halo Waters and One-Eye Jack had challenged a drunken bullwhacker to an arm-wrestling contest at the bar, while Whiskey-guts Ryan was dedicatedly demolishing yet another bottle.

Suddenly Joshua Vincent, Grat and their ranchhands burst through the swing doors and faced them and the din, as quickly, ceased.

'What have ye done with my daughter, Saunders?' Joshua bellowed. 'We know you got her.'

'Your daughter?' Matt echoed. 'You mean Harriet? What should I want with her?'

'She's gone missing. And my neice Polly. Don't crawfish me. I know you got 'em.'

'What? This is the first I've heard about—'

'Yeah,' Mustang Ben roared. 'We can vouch for that. We met up with Matt miles away this marnin'. He's been out hunting all day.'

'Keep your nose outa this, you ugly-looking piece of offal,' Joshua snarled. 'This is between me and Saunders. Or maybe his brother.'

Suddenly Matt's heart sank at the thought of Jeb, but Mustang Ben was growling: 'I might not be the purtiest person on this planet, but I ain't a liar. You better take your words back, you white-haired old freak, or answer to me.'

'Yeah,' One-Eye Jack was fiddling with the Smith & Wesson self-cocker he had bought from Gus. 'Or me.'

This sentiment was affirmed by the Mexican *ciboleros* who had got to their feet, bristling with anger, preparing for action.

Joshua Vincent was taken aback by the reinforcements Saunders seemed to have suddenly gathered, and for the first time in many long years had his bluster dampened. 'All I want is my girls back and the culprits who've snatched 'em punished. These are hanging offences.'

'All right, Mustang, tell your boys to calm down,' Matt said. 'I'm as worried as you are, Mr Vincent, specially about Polly for personal reasons. We'll do everything we can to help you find them. The sooner we start the better.

'Wait a minute,' Grat shouted, 'what's this about *personal reasons*? You keep your hands off my cousin, you lousy, thievin' polecat.'

'You're the stinkin' thieves, from what I've heard,' One-Eye sang out. 'Tryin' every trick to steal Matt Saunders's land.'

'You shut your big mouth,' Grat replied.

'Oops!' One-Eye cried, as he he winked hard at his pals and his left eye, made of marble, popped out, revealing a bare red socket, and rolled disconcertingly along the bar.

Simultaneously the Smith & Wesson in his hand spat lead, the slug searing through the flesh of Grat's thigh, knocking him with a sledgehammer blow off his feet and he collapsed, screaming.

The Mexicans immediately sprang into action, crashing over tables to shield themselves, revolvers sending warning shots around the Tarantula bunch who were caught wrongfooted, backed up against the wall.

'OK! Easy!' Matt shouted, his Peacemaker out. 'We don't want a bloodbath.'

'Yah,' Mustang agreed. 'Hold it, boys. I think these tree rats have got the message. Me an' my *compañeros* don't take kindly to insults.'

'All right,' Vincent growled, glancing at Grat. 'Ya've got yourself some fancy shootists, Saunders.

Two can play at that game. There'll be a reckoning.'

'Dang me!' One-Eye drawled, reaching for his marble eye to shove it back in the socket. 'Thass the trouble with these trick guns. I'm durned if it didn't go off accidental!'

FIFTEEN

Suddenly the saloon's swing doors burst open and Polly stepped in, supporting the bedraggled Harriet and followed sheepishly by Curly.

'She's all right,' Polly cried. 'She's been through hell, but she's OK.'

'What's happened to you, girl?' Joshua demanded. 'Where you been? We been worried sick.'

'Where've *you* been?' Harriet turned to look at her father, accusingly. 'I've been waiting all day and half the night for you to rescue me.'

She staggered past him and threw her arms around Matthew's neck, sobbing with her face against his chest. Taken aback, he could do little else but put a comforting arm around her and pat her shoulder. 'You're safe now, Harriet,' he said.

'I asked what happened to you!' her father roared.

'I been raped,' Harriet bawled. 'Raped and beaten over and over again.'

110

'What?' Joshua's long white hair hung about his grim face as he gawped at her. 'What you talking about girl?'

'Matt, I'm sorry,' Harriet wailed, holding up her bleeding wrists to show him. 'They had me tied. I couldn't stop them. I ain't as pure as the virgin snow no more but I'm still the same girl. You still want me, don't you?'

'What?' Joshua croaked, his mouth agape.

Matt tried to release himself from her embrace. 'You've got the wrong idea, Harri, I've never said anything about wanting you.'

'Please, Matt,' Harriet wailed. 'Take me home with you.'

'What?' Joshua repeated. 'Has he been making promises to you?'

'She's upset,' Matt said. 'Girls, bring her a chair.'

When Alice did so and Polly tried to soothe the girl, Harriet waved her away. 'Git your hands off me, cousin. I know what you're up to.'

'Talk some sense, girl. Who raped you?'

'Them two,' Harriet sniffled, as Curly discreetly withdrew a step behind his ranch boss.

'Who?' Joshua raged, bewildered, uncaring, that the whole town would hear them.

'Who?' Harriet blinked tearful eyes at him as she sipped from a glass of water. 'Jeb, of course.'

'Jeb Riley?'

'Yes, he's dead back at the crik.'

'Dead?' Matt echoed, shocked. 'Who killed him?'

'I did,' Curly timidly volunteered. 'He was making her do things she didn't like. I shot him down. We was in Wildcat Canyon. He told me we'd get a big ransom and be rich. You'll be gettin' Jeb's letter in the morning . . . Mr Vincent, sir.'

'You raped me, too, that first time,' Harriet accused.

'But you said—' The boy turned to her, pleading. 'You said if I helped you get away we'd be wed. You promised.'

'You stupid boy. That was just a trick,' Harriet growled. 'Why should I want to wed you? I'm Matthew's gal. The truth is you still raped me, Curly, didn't you?'

'Is that right, boy?' Joshua hollered. 'Draw, you varmint.'

Polly tried to intervene, screaming. 'He saved her. I was there! Jeb was belting her something terrible and Curly shot him. No!'

Daisy bulkily held her back for her own safety as Joshua jerked out his old Colt .45 from his belt. Too late the startled Curly went for his pistol. 'I'm sorry,' he whimpered, before the first bullet hit him. He went down and Vincent stood over him, firing bullets into his head and body until all six had gone.

Nobody, apart from Polly, tried to stop him. The men and women, too, just stood and stared at the execution. By the law of the West this was the punishment any man who abused a decent woman, or even an indecent one, should expect to have meted out to him.

'Serve him right,' Grat groaned, as he lay on the floor holding his blood-soaked leg.

The saloon was silent as the acrid black powder smoke drifted. 'Come on, girl,' Joshua ordered. 'Saunders don't want you. We're taking you and Grat home.'

'Oh my God!' Polly cried. 'What a dreadful business. Why didn't any of you stop him?'

Mustang and the other men shrugged and turned to the bar as the Tarantula men took away the wounded Grat.

Matt touched Polly gently on the shoulder. 'You'd better go with your uncle.'

'I don't want to,' she murmured. 'They may be kin of mine but I don't like those people. Why, Matthew? Why do you have to have all this killing?'

He shrugged, 'I didn't start it. I knew Jeb had a lot of wildness in him but I didn't know he was real evil. I'm going to go see if I can find him.'

Polly avoided his eyes and said stubbornly, 'I'm not going back with them. I'll find myself a job in town as a waitress or something.'

'Gus,' Matt shouted. 'Give her a cup of coffee.' He patted her shoulder. 'Stay here. I'll be back.'

The bloody execution of Curly had sobered Mustang

Ben and his men, who headed back to the ranch.

The smoke had drifted out through the doorway and could be seen in the moonlight floating across the street up into the dark spruces on the mountain-side. Gus Brown was mournfully inspecting a shattered window, sweeping up bits of broken glass, tossing disjointed tables out of the door and, when Curly had been hauled out on his journey to Boot Hill, he covered the bloody path on the floorboards with sawdust.

'Why me?' he moaned again. 'Why can't they go do their target practice someplace else? Something's gotta be done; this has become the most unsafe town in the whole of Washoe county.'

Over in a corner Polly Vincent was being 'com-forted' by Alice and the fulsome Daisy, although they were probing more for any juicy gossip about the rape at Wildcat Canyon. Gus poked Leonara in her ribs and muttered, 'Maybe this is our chance to recruit pretty Polly to our ranks. Go and give her some friendly persuasion.'

'Aw, she ain't that sorta gal.'

'You never know. Go lay it on thick.'

'Didn't you see any of what they were doin' to Horrible Harriet?' Alice was asking. 'I've a right to know. Jeb had promised to marry me.'

'He was larruping her with his belt, that's all I saw, Polly replied, as she sipped her mug of coffee. 'I've told you.'

'Now then, girls, don't pester Polly. She's been through an ordeal herself,' Leonara butted in, giving a wink to Daisy. 'Now she's all alone at the mercy of the world; no family, no friends, no fortune. You ain't gonna get nowhere with Matt Saunders, Polly. He's a loner. Sometimes I think he must be lacking his passionate parts.'

'In my opinion he's one of them pansies,' Daisy opined. 'I've tried. Not a flicker. You don't need him, honey. A good-looking gal like you can git any red-blooded man in the county.'

'Yes, she's a real bobby-dazzler, ain't she?' Alice joined in, stroking Polly's hair out of her eyes. 'Just look at these luxuriant, silken, raven locks. She could make a fortune if she stayed with us.'

'Reminds me of myself back in the forty-niner days,' Leonara remarked, giving her a gummy smile. 'Them California miners – wow! I was raking in a thousand dollars a night in gold dust.'

'So, how come you've ended up old and broke in this hellhole,' Polly responded indignantly, as she refused a glass of bourbon and a cigarette they tried to press on her. 'I don't mean to be rude, but I hope you're not suggesting that I should follow in, frankly, your far from fragrant footsteps.'

'Aw, in them days it was easy come, easy go.' Leonara gave one of her nonchalant, fluttery waves. 'Foolish of me, I admit. I should have invested in a little whorehouse of my own. But what's to stop you,

Polly? I've noticed you've got your head stuck on right. A classy gal like you could make a mint. Stash it away in the bank and purty soon you'd be a young lady of independent means. You could open a milliner's shop of your own.'

Alice patted Polly's knee. 'Ol' Gus is OK. He'll let you keep a quarter of what you make. Then there's tips from grateful customers and a bonus on busy nights. It's a fun life, sweetheart. You just don't know 'til you try. What ya gonna earn down the street serving in the pie shop – a dollar a week an' your keep? Here the sky's the limit. Believe me, babe.'

Polly, startled by their attentions, protested, 'That's not just me, I'm afraid. I believe in love and marriage I—'

'Hark at her,' Daisy scoffed. 'Love an' marriage. Out on some rundown ranch in the back of beyond working your fingers to the bone, flattened by a big, fat, hairy husband like Grat every night. All he wants is to get his oats for free.'

'Perhaps you've never done it before,' Leonara remarked, cosyin' up close. 'But once you do you'll find it's easy. Nothing to it. Gracious! What more could a young gal want than spend her days in a cosy saloon while the blizzard howls outside. Haven't you any pity for the poor lonesome cowboys and the old guys who believe they're past it? You, Polly, would be bringing moments of passion and pleasure into their lives. Ours is really a saintly occupation, doing good

116

for all mankind.'

'Yeah.' Alice wrinkled her nose, gave a growl of pleasure and nudged her. 'What more could a gal want than to spend her days in idle drunken debauchery, as I believe that great thinker the Markee dee Sade said.'

'We're giving you good advice in your present circumstances.' Leonara stroked a long, scarlet nail across Polly's cheek in a threatening way. 'Honey, it's cold outside. Go have a word with Gus. He'll fix you up a bed.'

'I feel strange,' Polly murmured, weakening. 'I don't know—'

'Sure, darling,' Daisy urged. 'You an' me, we could be best friends. I'll show ya the ropes. You sleep here tonight.'

SIXTEEN

The throbbing pain in his chest intensified when he tried to move, but Jeb Riley knew he had to get out of the canyon. So this was what it was like getting shot? Like a ton weight hitting him, tearing through him, knocking him unconscious. They must have panicked in their hurry to escape failing to check whether he was dead or alive. When he regained consciousness all was quiet, the horses gone. He had tried to plug the wound with his bandanna. He had crawled back into the dug out and retrieved his Winchester; there were fifteen rounds in the magazine. Jeb used the carbine as a crutch to get to his feet and took unsteady steps down through the ravine. He must reach town under cover of darkness, steal a horse and get back to the safety of the ranch.

But a wave of nausea hit him, spinning his mind and he crashed down into the undergrowth. 'I shoulda killed her first thing, that crafty bitch,' he muttered. 'And him too, that treacherous li'l rat.' Jeb lay there, breathing hard, aware of the blood-stickiness of his shirt. 'I gotta get on my feet.'

Too late! He heard the sound of horses' thudding hoofs, men's voices. He scrabbled through the loose earth, crawling towards a more advantageous position. Let 'em come, he thought.

Joshua Vincent had commandeered a buggy and ordered two of his men to take Grat and Harriet home. Then he had charged off at a gallop at the head of his men towards Wildcat Canyon.

'You think he's still up there?' his ramrodder, Dusty Stevens, asked, peering up into the shadowy ravine.

Joshua sat his horse like a general at the forefront of battle. 'There's only one way to find out.'

Dusty, short and lean as a jockey, jumped from his mustang. 'Come on, boys. Let's take a look. Spread out and step quiet, OK?'

From behind a fallen stump Jeb Riley listened and watched. Suddenly he saw dark shapes creeping up through the scrubby alders towards him. In the lead was a small, skinny man coming on at a crouch, his pistol raised. Jeb lined up the sights of the carbine on him, squeezed the trigger and the bullet cracked out hitting Dusty in the chest and bowling him over.

'Ooh!' the ramrodder cried, like a man who might have stubbed his toe. But it was the last sound he ever made.

Jeb grinned, wolfishly, levering another slug into the spout. 'It's as easy as potting rabbits.' He panted with the effort, a killing wildness in him, and three more punchers had their lives snuffed out. Others hit the ground or turned and ran as the Winchester's lead caroomed past their heads.

Matthew Saunders heard the sound waves of the shots bouncing away off the walls of Wild Cat ravine as he rode up in the wake of the Vincent men. 'Oh God!' he cried to himself. 'He's still shooting.'

Urged on by Joshua, his remaining men had sought cover, blamming away with carbines and revolvers at the flashes of fire from the Winchester. But it was difficult to get a bead on Riley in the dark.

'Crawl up round the back of him,' the old patriarch shouted. 'Flush him out.'

Matt leapt from his mustang and ran up to join them, unable to guess in the noise of gunfire how many Jeb had left in his magazine. But there was a sudden lull and silence reigned as the gunsmoke drifted.

'Jeb,' Matt shouted, as he knelt down among the men. 'Throw down your guns. It's me, Matt. I'll make sure you get a fair trial.'

'You're joking,' Vincent grunted, but hoped the words might lure Riley out.

The pain in his chest tore through him as Jeb pulled the Winchester into his shoulder. Gritting his teeth he levered the last bullet into the breech and thumbed the hammer. Suddenly the clouds parted and in the moonlight he had a clear view of Vincent in his black frock coat, his white hair flailing from beneath his Stetson, as he sat his startled charger, rifle in hand.

'Goodbye old man.' Jeb's bullet spat out unerringly and with grim satisfaction he saw Joshua throw up his hands and topple off his horse. 'Go play ya harp.'

'Oh no!' Matt ran back to the fallen man, but Joshua's eyes were bulging, staring at him. He was trying to speak but black blood spurted from his mouth and he fell back. 'He's dead,' Matt sighed.

A couple of the punchers gathered around, their eyes worried, for with the rancher, his son and the ramrodder, all gone, plus other men dead and wounded, they were at a loss as to what to do, the fight knocked out of them.

Matt left Vincent with them and shouted out, 'Jeb! I'm coming up.'

His half-brother crawled forward to meet him, his eyes crazed, his mouth open, one hand reaching out, pleading. 'Matt, I killed him for *you*. Joshua's dead, ain't he?'

The young rancher gripped his hand, frowning. 'Yes, he's dead.'

'We've won,' Riley coughed out. 'Doncha see? I did right, didn't I?'

'I dunno,' Matt mused. 'But it's over now.'

121

There was a deafening burst of gunfire in his ears; three of the punchers had climbed up beside them and were emptying their revolvers into Jeb's face and body.

He fell back, writhing and twisting until he was finally still. Matthew reached over and closed his eyes. 'You damn fool kid,' he whispered.

'It sure is over now,' an older one of the cowhands gruffly repeated. 'We oughta kill you, too, Saunders, but what's the use?'

It was getting late by the time Matt rode back into Washoe City. The stores were closed and shuttered as was the saloon door, but there was a light on inside so Matt hammered with his fist. Nobody answered so he looked through a window. The girls seemed to be gathered around Polly Vincent and Gus was helping her to her feet, a burly arm about her, leading her to the back rooms.

The young rancher went round to the back door and kicked it in. The big, brawny saloonkeeper was in the corridor, pushing the girl into one of the bedrooms. He blinked with surprise.

'What's going on?' Matt demanded.

'Nuthin',' Gus Brown blustered. 'She ain't feelin' well. We're letting her sleep here.'

'Oh yeah?' He stepped forward. The girl was slumped in Brown's arms, her eyes closed, only half-conscious. He caught hold of her chin, shook her hard and her eyelids flickered open. 'What you been slipping her?'

'Matt,' Polly murmured. 'I feel so strange. I just want to sleep.'

'We haven't touched her,' Leonara screeched, in support of her pimp. 'She just come over funny. We was gonna let her share Daisy's bed.'

'Yeah, an' then what? Come on.' The rancher caught hold of Polly and swept her up in his arms. 'We're getting outa here.'

At the back door he turned and met Gus's eyes again. 'You ever touch this gal again, I'll kill you.'

'What have I done?' Gus protested. 'She's a free agent. She can sleep where she likes.'

'Yeah,' Leonara drawled. 'We were doing you a favour. We didn't know you had designs on the gal.'

'Yes,' Daisy tittered. 'We thought you was one of *them.*'

Matt scowled at them. 'You heard what I said. You ever so much as speak to Polly again you better go for your guns.'

He turned on his heel and carried her through the darkness along the hardened mud street.

Polly hooked her arm around his neck. 'Matt?' she murmured, 'where are we going? What are you doing with me?'

'Mrs McGinty's got a back room in her boarding house. I called in on her 'fore I came to the saloon. It's poky, but you'll be OK.'

There were lamps burning in the boarding house and he pushed inside. 'Here she is,' he called, taking her through. He lay her gently on the small cot. 'She's feelin' dozy, but she'll be all right. She just needs to sleep.'

'I hope so,' Mrs McGinty squawked. 'I don't want no invalids staying here. I got enough to do.'

'Thank you, Matt,' Polly whispered, touching his cheek. 'Thank you for getting me away from those people. They were making horrible suggestions to me.'

'You sleep now,' he replied. 'I've paid your board for one week. I'll call in on Saturday.'

'I'll pay you back,' the girl whispered before she sank into a deep slumber, '. . . one day.'

SEVENTEEN

The wild horses roamed the mountainous high country of Montana and Wyoming. They had wide eyes and short ears and were mostly dun in colour. They gained what nourishment they could from the silver sage and scrub. In winter their coats grew long and thick, but even so, as the snow covered the slopes and blizzards raged, temperatures plummeting to thirty degrees below on the Fahrenheit scale, many succumbed to famine and cold. Pumas too were an ever present danger, waiting to pounce at the horses' watering holes; spring foals were often on the big cats' menus. At mating time the stallions became as violent as the storms that thundered through the passes. They would battle for days, kicking and tearing with their teeth, inflicting severe injuries to gain mastery of the herd.

Such a one was the black stallion who, until Mustang Ben and his men arrived, had been the supreme master of his herd of mares, sub-dominant males, colts, yearlings and foals. His scars were evidence of battle. Now he was in solitary confinement, stomping around the corral, stepping with a proud action, his head held high, his tail lifted and twitching angrily, calling out with high-pitched whinnies to the alpha mare and the others who had been dragged from him.

'We've broke most of t'others to the saddle,' Mustang Ben mused, as they watched. 'But we got a fight on our hands with him.'

'I don't want you to be too hard on him, Ben,' Matt said. 'Leave some spirit in him.'

He had seen mustangs cruelly treated too often. Some wranglers would even leave a horse all night with its back leg held up by weights, whipped and beaten and tortured until all fight was gone.

'A hoss is like a woman,' One-Eye commented. 'They need a good beating now and again so they remember who's boss.'

'I ain't so sure about that,' Matt replied quietly. 'I've seen the way the Sioux do it. They sorta coax the creature up close, blow gently in its nostrils, stroke its back until it gets used to the touch and then kinda just slip aboard for a bit, no trouble. I've even seen 'em walk away and the hoss will docilely follow. Real strange.'

Whiskey-guts Ryan, who was leaning on the rail alongside them, gave a bellow of contemptuous laughter. 'Go on, pal, try whispering in that bastard's ear. He'll bite your nose off.'

The tall Texan, Halo Waters, joined in the merriment. 'You might be able to whisper sweet nuthin's into his shell-like by the time we've finished with him, but first we've gotta break him. There's no other way.'

He gave a yell of excitement as he leapt over the rail, followed by Mustang Ben and One-Eye, who sent lariats spinning about the stallion's head and hoofs to drag him kicking and fighting to an eye-rolling, trembling halt. When Halo threw a saddle over his back he leapt away instinctively believing it to be a puma leaping from ambush upon him. His three tormentors dragged him back and Halo managed to cinch the saddle tight and get a bridle over his head, the cruel spade bit between his teeth pressing down on his tongue.

'Ride him!' Mustang hollered, as One-Eye leapt into the saddle, the ropes were released and the lanky horsebreaker spun the stallion to go careering around the corral. The watching Mexicans screamed advice as the stallion kicked for the sky, going into a series of twisting, bucking spins, tossing One-Eye back and forth like a rag doll.

'Look at the daylight 'tween One-Eye's pants an' the saddle at every bounce,' Whiskey-guts chortled. 'Them two's gonna part company any second now.'

And so it proved true as the stallion gave a mighty

leap to throw this man-wildcat from him and One-Eye juddered every bone in his body as he hit the dust hard. 'Ouf!' But now the wrangler was in real trouble as the horse turned on him and tried to stomp him into the dirt.

Mustang Ben and Halo had to holler and slap at the rabid horse to distract him until they could get ropes on him and he came to another outraged halt.

'You wanna try whispering to him now, Matt?' Mustang jeered.

He scoffed in surprise when Matt replied, 'Yes, I think I will,' and jumped over the rail. He filled a bucket with water from the trough just outside the corral and cautiously approached. He held up a hand to silence the shrilling Latinos. 'Give me a chance, boys. He's my horse. I've bought him from you and I've a right to try a little experiment.'

'*Sí, muchachos*,' Mustang repeated, with a grin of his protruding purple lips. 'Give him a break.'

'This's no way to break a hoss,' Halo complained. 'Where's the fun?'

But they watched in silence as Matt offered the water. The stallion backed away, his eyes wide and puzzled, but his nostrils twitched to the scent of it and gradually he was persuaded to drink. As he did so Matt reached out a hand to gently stroke his forehead although tensed to jump back from the bite he was half-expecting. The horse tossed his head, nervously, his tail still twitching indignantly, his ears

128

flattened back angrily, expecting another blow, danger and attack.

'I'd like you boys to back off now,' Matt said.

As they did so the horse seemed to calm and peered inquisitively at this man before him, the first of his kind to show him any mercy. 'Come on, boy,' Matt whispered, putting the bucket aside and reaching to stroke his neck. 'You and me are going to be pals.'

The stallion tossed his head and backed away, still quivering from the fight with One-Eye. He had already had the saddle removed and seemed calmer so Matt eased the bridle from his head, turned abruptly and walked away. The horse stood for moments, perplexed, then, realizing he was free, trotted off.

'I'd appreciate it if you'd let me handle him from now on,' Matt said. 'I'm gonna take it easy every day, getting closer to him bit by bit. Might even try the old Injin nostril-breathin' routine. What's the betting I'll have a saddle on him in a week or so and have him eating crackers outa my hand like ol' Crackers does?'

'I'll lay five dollars against on that,' Whiskey-guts growled, and the other wranglers yelled their bets.

'Looks like I might do well outa this.' Matt grinned, and said, 'Come on, you boys, how about helping me do a bit of proper work? Got some cows to catch.'

*

Since the shooting of Joshua Vincent an uneasy ceasefire reigned in the valley. Grat Vincent had suffered a thigh flesh wound which was healing well and until it was right he had taken to riding around in a four-wheel, low-neck carriage. In fact, he had been seen heading across the pass in it in the direction of Billings, or possibly Miles City.

Harriet was seething with longing for revenge, not just for the rape, but for her humiliation in front of the townsfolk now that Matthew Saunders had made it clear he preferred the company of her snake-in-the-grass cousin, Polly. What she had thought of as love for the young rancher had suddenly turned into a burning hatred. For both of them.

'I want vengeance, too,' her mother, Martha, told her, 'but too many men's been killed. While he's still got that gang of gunslingers on his payroll we're hog-tied.'

'I ain't so sure of that,' Harriet drawled. 'Why do you think Grat's gone to Miles City? We got a plan. You'll see.'

Her shocking experience had done little to quell her tomboy spirits and, in her fringed buckskins and chaps, she would often be away all day on her skewbald trying to keep a lookout from the hillsides on the Longbranch ranch to see what they were up to.

It was early on a Sunday morning when Matt came from his cabin and, looking over at the corral, saw

130

Halo Waters with a rope around the stallion's neck, cursing and shouting as he tried to get a saddle on him. By brute strength he dragged the horse close to him as Whiskey-guts and One-Eye cheered him on. He smashed his fist into the stallion's nose and lip making him scream with pain and rear up, flailing his hoofs and whinnying.

Matt vaulted the corral rail, caught Waters by his shoulder, spun him round and cracked his fist into his jaw, sending him sprawling. 'How do you like the same treatment?' he shouted.

Halo slowly got to his feet, glancing at his two companions, who had tensed, alert, and snarled, 'Who the hell you think you are?' Suddenly, true to his Texan instincts, he went for his gun, but Matt was seconds faster, his Peacemaker out of its greased holster, its bullet creasing Halo's knuckles, sending his .45 flying.

Matt spun around on the two other men, who were also reaching for their shooting irons. 'Go on,' he said, his left hand ready to fan the hammer. 'Try me.'

'That's enough!' Mustang Ben's voice hollered. 'Put your guns away, boys.' He strode across, his bulbous birthmarked head even more florid than usual. 'What the hell's going on?'

'Aw,' Halo whined, sucking at his bleeding knuckles, grimacing with agony. 'I was only going to show him how to ride his damn stallion. Why didn't you

131

kill him? Ye're s'posed to be my buddies.'

'There'll be no killing,' Mustang ordered, then tugged at his bushy beard, contemplating Matt. 'In fact, I've been thinking now thangs have quietened down, my friend Matthew don't really need our help no more. I think it's time we was moseying on.'

'No hard feelings,' Matt said, eyeing Halo, 'but I expressly told you I didn't want you messin' with the stallion. I wanna tame him my way.'

'I shouldn't think it's done much harm,' Mustang grinned. 'Look at it like the bad sheriff routine when he beats the shit outa ya, then his deputy comes in and plays the good guy to get ya to confess your misdeeds to him. When the hoss has simmered down he'll be glad to see ya, Matt.'

The Mexicans had joined them, joshing Halo callously for losing the draw. Mustang shouted orders and within ten minutes they had packed their bedrolls and scant belongings, and were ready to go. 'So long, *compadre*,' Mustang called from horseback. 'If you need me send for me.'

'Where you heading?'

'Some place a little livelier, perhaps. I'll be cashing your cheque come meatpacking time in Miles City. Might see you there. Good luck, *amigo*.'

With which, he spurred his mustang and charged out and away from the ranch shacks, followed by the yipping and yelling *ciboleros* and the three Americans.

'Whoo,' Dave drawled, as he watched them go.

'Thangs are gonna be bit quieter round here now.'

'Yeah,' Matt rejoined, although he didn't sound too sure. 'I hope so.'

EIGHTEEN

'Where you off to?' Dave asked, when Matt appeared later that morning, clean shaven and duded up in his Sunday suit and best bandanna. 'Goin' courtin'?'

'You could put it like that.' Matt gave him a grin as he swung on to Crackers. 'In the past I've been a love 'em an' leave 'em sorta fellow. But I have to admit I'm smitten. Take it easy, boys, I'll be back tonight.'

It was true. His heart leapt with joy like the prairie larks soaring in the sky at the prospect of seeing Polly again. This would be the third Sunday since the shoot-out at Wild Cat Canyon that he had ridden into town to meet her. She had found a job working at Poulson's store; Poulson's wife had a back problem and spent much of her time resting. Polly's knowhow of running a similar establishment in St Louis had proved a Godsend for them. She was busy every day bar Sunday.

Matt had brought Jeb's body back to the ranch to

bury down by the river, not because he had any great regard for him, but he was blood kin. In fact a lot of the recent burials might have been avoided if it had not been for Jeb's foolishness. He hoped Grat Vincent understood that and was prepared to let bye-gones be byegones. Nonetheless, he carried the Winchester carbine in his saddle boot just in case of trouble. It was easier to carry than the bulky Sharps with its forty-inch barrel and ten pounds in weight and of course, it was a fifteen shot.

Matt had avoided the saloon since the incident when, he was sure, Gus tried to drug the girl. There was nowhere much else to go in Washoe City on a Sunday, so as the weather was summery again, Polly usually packed them a picnic and they took a ride out in the mountains together.

She was waiting for him at the boarding house, smiling and radiant in her green velvet dress and a new, wide-brimmed straw sunhat. 'Hi,' she called, handing him the picnic basket, hitching up her skirts to reveal black stockings and bootees and climbing aboard the docile cow pony he had brought along for her. 'Where are we heading to,' Polly asked, 'the high country?'

'Sure, wherever you like,' Matt said, and they set off at a fast trot towards the Crazy Mountains.

'Hot damn,' Harriet cried, as, hidden behind rocks on a hilltop, she watched the couple through her eyeglass. 'I'm gonna have to do somethang about this. That woman needs attending to.'

'It's so wonderful to breathe fresh air and be out in the wide open spaces after being cooped up in the store all week.' Polly took big lungfuls of the sharp air as she sat beside him on a grassy slope and admired the vista of green hills and the distant snow-capped Rockies. 'I really love this country. What are those beautiful blue flowers?'

'Lupins, I guess,' he said more interested in what goodies she had brought in her lunch box. 'Molasses cookies. Wow! Did you cook 'em?'

'I must admit I did. But you're s'posed to start with a chicken leg. Here.' Polly passed one to him. 'Are you going to make a fire today and boil up some coffee.'

'Yeah, later on down in that wood there, maybe.'

'Oh dear, I hope you're not planning to take advantage of me.'

'You never know your luck, sweetheart.'

They laughed and chatted amiably as they ate, Polly asking him about his week, how he was pro-gressing with the stallion, and he told her about the trouble that morning. 'Mustang Ben and his boys didn't take kindly to me telling 'em how to tame a hoss. They've moved on and in a way I'm relieved. They were eating us out of house and home.'

'When are you going to show me your home?'

'It ain't much. Just a coupla rooms, but I've got the

walls caulked and it can be kinda cosy,' he said. 'It's missing a woman's touch.'

'Are you looking for one?' Polly wiped her lips with a napkin and lay back staring at a hawk hovering in the blue sky. 'I don't want to push you, but it would be nice to know if you are serious about me. I mean—'

For an answer he embraced her and kissed her lips deep and long. 'You got eyes the colour of sage after fresh rain,' he said as he twirled a lock of her hair in his finger and studied her sadly. 'I *would* like you to be my woman but. . . .'

'But what?'

He sat up to lean on one elbow. 'For a start it's all very well saying how wonderful it is right now in the spring. But there's a long, hard winter in these parts. Temperature drops way below, even minus sixty sometimes. It's lambswool socks, long johns and muskrat hat weather. And that's only for going to bed. I'm not sure a gal like you's cut out for it.'

'You'd be warmer cuddled up with me than on your own.'

'And then, I ain't sure this trouble's blown over. Joshua Vincent was a man of the feud. I got a feelin' Grat and that madcap Harriet are the same, itching to avenge him.'

'So?' Polly turned to stroke his cheek. 'If we're wed I won't be a Vincent. I'll be a Saunders. I want to be with you, stand beside you whatever happens.'

'In that case,' he grinned, 'maybe we'd better go into Billings and roust up a preacher.'

Polly was looking a trifle tousled from the lovemaking as they came from the wood sometime later. 'You aren't kidding me are you, Matt?'

'I wouldn't kid you, Polly,' he said. 'We've both known since that time we first met that this was going to happen, haven't we? It's a damn sight better than my wildest dreams. We'll go find that preacher man next weekend, I promise you.'

'I don't care whether we're wed or not. I just want to be with you. But I suppose it would be nice.'

The sun was sinking fast as they rode back to town. 'Do you ever get the feeling we're being watched?' she asked.

Matt had seen the sun glinting on a rifle barrel or telescope up on the mountainside. 'I've an idea it's that crazy cousin of yourn.'

'Harriet? Doesn't she ever give up?'

'Hell hath no fury,' he muttered, 'as a woman scorned. Thank God she ain't exactly a crack shot.'

NINETEEN

Grat Vincent headed south to join the Bozeman Trail rather than cross the bumpy prairie in his low-necked carriage, flicking his whip across the backs of his pair of dappled greys and bowling along the banks of the Yellowstone through Billings and on to Junction City. He had packed a Remington rolling block rifle and a couple of revolvers because raiding parties of Sitting Bull's warriors were making sorties south from their camps over the Canadian border; settlers had been killed and stock stolen. But the only hold-up he encountered was a vast herd of buffalo streaming north on their annual migration. All he could do was sit there and watch them for half an hour as they crossed the trail.

Miles City was *en fête* with bunting and banners, an army brass band from Fort Keogh leading a parade through the packed streets, for the first locomotive of the railroad had arrived and was standing at the end of the track, resplendently, hissing and growling as speeches of welcome were made and fireworks exploded into the air.

The town's fourteen saloons, three dance halls and 'houses of cheer' in its Street of Sin were crowded as hundreds of excited squaddies, cowboys and bull-whackers clamoured to quench both of their thirsts. Ranchers and their families from outlying districts had also flocked in and Russell's roller skating rink, and the Cosmopolitan theatre were packed out.

The arrival of the Northern Pacific Railroad meant that the traders and their frontier customers would no longer have to rely on the annual arrival of the steamboats on the spring high water or the slow progress of jerk-line, twelve-horse-power wagon trains along the freight trails, or the even slower 'hay-fuelled' bull wagons. Now the stores could be stocked with essentials and luxuries alike.

Already Jordan's store was displaying shelves of foreign wines, fine liquors and cigars, the latest in gents' and ladies' fashions, rubber goods, new-fangled agricultural implements, canned goods and wooden casks of Falk's and Schlitz's 'celebrated Milwaukee lager' that crowds were clamouring to buy.

Remittance man Sydney Paget was strutting around in his ornate, redcoat British uniform with a white pith helmet, and a monocle in his eye, organizing the horse races just outside town, and generally being taken for a ride himself by the canny contenders on their cowponies jostling to take part.

All in all it was an amazing sight to Grat, who found the brick-built Merchants and Drovers' Bank was open for business in spite of the public holiday and that his father was much wealthier than he had dreamed. As son and heir he would inherit it all. Women didn't have much in the way of rights in Montana and his mother and Harriet would be reliant on his providing for them.

Grat's next call was to the office of the *Yellowstone Journal* where he explained to the editor, Sam Gordon, that he had come on behalf of the citizens of Washoe City to pick up replies to their advertisement for a lawman.

'You got a dozen,' Sam replied, 'so you shouldn't have much trouble taming your town.'

'Yeah,' Grat vaguely muttered, looking through them. 'Thanks.' Once outside he tore them up and let them blow away on the breeze.

'I'm looking for a man named Jake Rigney,' Grat shouted above the din in Charley Brown's saloon.

Charley was ladling out whiskey from an open barrel beneath the bar into half-pint mugs as fast as his assistant could grab cash from grasping hands. 'He ain't here,' he yelled. 'Try the Cottage. Or he might be at the races or in Poker Nell's, who knows?'

Charley grabbed a wooden bull yoke and cracked

it across the skull of a jackleg who had began a brawl with a bunch of cowboys. 'Go fight outside,' he roared, and returned to his task.

'Thanks,' Grat said again, and shouldered his way outside and across the street to the two-storey Cottage with a false front that gave the impression of a third floor. But Rigney had been and gone. Six saloons later Grat tracked him down to the Steamboat which was more of a gambling hell, curtains drawn day and night, whale oil lamps flickering, roulette, keno, blackjack and a game of stud poker in full sway.

'That's him,' a waitress gal in a short skirt pointed out. 'But I wouldn't disturb him if I were you. He's got a terrible temper.'

Jake Rigney was broadbacked, in a cutaway camel-coloured coat, neat pants over fancy, high-heeled boots, clean linen and a cravat. His long blond hair was slicked back and his ruddy face had a clean-shaven, resolute look. Apart from his strong jowls and hefty, dimpled chin, there was little to suggest he was the sort of man Grat needed.

Until, that was, a black gent, powerfully-built and sporting a satin waistcoat and white cowboy hat, sat opposite him in the poker game gave a grinning leer and began to rake in the pot of notes, silver and gold coins. Rigney reached out with his right hand to grip his opponent's wrist and brought out a two-shot der-ringer in his left. As the black man went for a knife, two shots cracked out and he collapsed back, gripping his bleeding shoulder, grimacing with pain. Rigney shrugged, scooped up the pot and tipped the cash into his coat pockets.

As he turned, with a look of disdain, away from the game Grat caught his arm, and said, 'Are you the man my father, Joshua Vincent, sent for?'

Rigney nodded. 'You've taken your time. You were s'posed to meet me a fortnight ago.'

'We've been indisposed. Pa's dead. And' – he tapped his thigh – 'I caught a packet. But we still require your services.'

'We'd better talk outside,' Rigney said, lighting a cheroot.

Grat limped after him and remarked to the waitress, 'I see what you mean.' Hair trigger, he thought. He might be just our man.

Rigney led the way along to McQueen House and indicated two chairs on the veranda. 'The deal proposed by your old man was five hundred up front and five hundred on completion.'

'Hey, you gunslingers don't come cheap, do ya?'

'If you don't like it, do your own killing.'

Grat gave a faint smile. 'I'd rather you did it for me.' He pulled out a wallet and counted out five hundred in greenbacks. A waiter stood gawping, eyes popping at the sight of the cash. Grat ordered coffee and waited until he had gone. 'We just need one man killing. He's canny and reputed to be fast. But I've an idea we can do it without any risk to ourselves.'

'How's that?' Rigney grunted.

Grat winked. 'I got a plan. We'll leave tomorrow in my carriage. I'll explain on the way. Meanwhile I think I'll book in here overnight. Who are all these people arriving?'

'There's some sorta banquet on. Railroad men, army officers and their ladies, various nobs and town nobodies who think they're somebodies.' Rigney eased the derringer out of his left sleeve and detached it from a contraption around his forearm. 'Guess I better reload. Never know when I might need this.'

'Amazing,' Grat bellowed. 'You just drop it down into your palm when you need it?'

'Yep. Or use this.' Rigney opened his coat to reveal a revolver shoulder-holstered under his right armpit. 'Being left-handed gives me a slight advantage too. The surprise element.'

'You and that black man? They've got a sheriff here, ain't they? Aren't you bothered he might come after you?'

'It was a fair fight. He asked for it. Anyway, he ain't dead. Who gives a shit about a damn darkie? But you've got a point. Maybe I'd better be moving on.'

'Don't worry, Mr Rigney,' Grat grinned. 'We don't have a sheriff in Washoe City. You'll be our first one.'

TWENTY

Although they had, as yet, had no replies to their advertisement in the *Yellowstone Journal* for a sheriff the newly-formed Washoe City council held a meeting to discuss his remuneration and duties when appointed.

Horace Poulson proposed that he, himself, should be elected mayor. 'This onerous duty I'm willing to take on, unless any others wish to stand,' he told a crowded public meeting.

This agreed, Poulson went on to propose that cash should be collected to pay for a jail and sheriff's office to be built. Just a solid pine-log cabin.

'Only men are entitled to vote on such matters,' he somewhat pompously pointed out to Polly Vincent, who had raised a hand with the rest of them when he asked for approval.

'But Wyoming has given women the right to vote at both national and local elections,' she replied.

'Don't you have any women's rights in Montana?'

'We did have a woman back in the '40s pioneered for women's rights,' oldtimer Horace Hickson fluted in his high-pitched squawk. 'Flora Tristan she was called, kept going on about emancipation, forming a Workers' Union and somebody called Karl Marx an' his manifesto.'

'So, what happened?' Polly asked.

'Her husband shot her,' Horace replied. 'She talked too much.'

When he got back to the Tarantula Ranch Grat Vincent was greeted with the welcome news that Mustang Ben and his fast-shooters had hightailed it out of Washoe County.

'They didn't look like they would be coming back,' Harriet drawled with relish. 'So now's our chance to corner them lousy polecats. I wanna be in on it.'

'Who's the bloodthirsty little vixen?' Rigney asked.

'Aw, she's my sister. You'll get used to her,' Grat said. 'But this means your job is gonna be a piece of cake. Come on, no time like the present, let's head into town with the boys.'

'Yee-hagh!' Harriet screamed. 'I'm riding with ya. All I want is revenge on them who kilt my daddy.'

When they charged into Washoe City they found the town meeting in full swing. Grat stomped up to the mayor's table and, shoving Poulson aside, called out, 'Gentlemen, I want to introduce your new sheriff, Mr Jake Rigney.'

Rigney ambled forward, smoking a cheroot, stepping through the crowded chairs and tables as if he had all the time in the world, joining Grat. 'Howdy, folks,' he drawled, tossing his blond hair out of his eyes. 'I can assure you I'll soon have this town tamed.'

'But,' Poulson stuttered. 'We have had no other applicants.'

'There ain't none,' Grat lied. 'I've been to Miles City, spoke to the editor of the *Journal* and he warmly recommends Jake here. There weren't no other replies to your ad, so I'm proposing Jake for the job. All in favour?'

There was a confused murmur and Grat banged the table with his pistol butt. 'Right, that's carried. I can tell you that Mr Rigney has served bravely as marshal at Abilene, Denver and Dodge City. He's risked his life cleaning up those towns so Washoe ain't gonna be a problem.'

'Just a minute,' barber Katzenjammer protested. 'I voz in Abilene long time. I never hear of no marshal called Rigney.'

'So, just why did *you* come West?' Grat asked. 'It wouldn't be anythang to do with a spot of fraudulent business you got mixed up with back in Boston, by any chance? Maybe our new sheriff should investigate *you*?'

The German's jaw dropped, his eyes staring. His

name like many men's was an alias. Katzenjammer was German for hangover – or 'the wailing of cats in one's head'. He had thought it amusing. But how did they find out about him? He looked far from amused now.

Poulson rose to intervene, crying, 'What the barber means is that this is undemocratic. You have no right—'

The burly Grat pushed him aside. 'Sit down and shut up, big mouth. If you wanna stay mayor you better watch out. Right, everybody, the meeting's over. You all support our new sheriff you'll be in safe hands.'

'Yeah, you can count on that,' Rigney hollered. 'The only people I don't like are troublemakers and they generally end up dead. So, who fancies a drink and joining me in a li'l game of poker?'

But most of the ordinary townspeople looked cowed and uneasy when they saw Grat's men lined up at the back of the room, among them two notorious villains, Ned Blair and Luther White, who he had enrolled at Billings as replacements for his lost cowhands. Most clattered their chairs aside and headed for the door, shamefacedly followed by Poulson and Polly.

'Keep an eye on them two, Harriet,' Grat said. 'Make sure they don't try to contact Matthew Saunders.'

'Shall I kill 'em now?' Harriet asked, eagerly.

'No, just make sure they turn in for the night. I don't want her killed,' Grat muttered in an insistent undertone. 'That girl is gonna be my wife one of these days pretty soon whether she likes it or not. Just watch her, thassall.'

'I'll watch that bitch 'til hell freezes over,' Harriet snarled. 'There's no way she's gonna be Matt's woman.'

Sunday dawned sunny and bright and Matt was more than eager to saddle Crackers and ride in to meet Polly. The town was eerily quiet, but that did not faze him for he was early. He hitched his horse to the rail and walked along the high sidewalk. A stranger, smartly attired, with long blond hair was leaned against the wall outside Poulson's store. He grimaced his strong jowls in a flashing smile. 'When's this joint open?' he asked. 'I'm hungry.'

'They don't open on the sabbath,' Matt replied, knocking at the door. 'But I'll ask inside. They might be able to fix you up with some bread and ham.'

The store door opened as if Polly was about to greet him, but she had a noose around her neck and a knife held to her throat by Harriet Vincent.

'Hiya, Matt,' Harriet growled in her deepest *basso profundo*. 'Come to find your simpering li'l sweetheart?'

Matt met Polly's distraught eyes, glimpsed the startled Poulsons behind her as a gun was thrust into his back and the stranger said, 'Make a move, mister, and I'll blast your spine apart.'

Expertly Rigney removed Matt's Peacemaker from its holster and stuck it in his belt. 'I'm the new sheriff of this town, pal, and I'm arresting you. Get your wrists behind you, fast.'

'Don't try anything, Matthew,' Harriet warned, 'or Polly Wolly Doodle gits it. I'll slit her like a pig. I'd gladly do so, but my brother plans to wed her. That might be more fun havin' her back at the ranch to torment, eh, Polly? One thang's fer sure, Matt Saunders, *you* won't be havin' her.'

'Don't be a fool, Harri. Let her go.' He put his hands back and felt the stranger twist twine about them, hard. 'You don't need Polly. You've got me.'

'We sure have,' Rigney said. 'Say your last goodbye, feller.'

'I'm sorry, Matt,' Polly cried. 'I tried to ride to warn you but Harri was waiting in the stable. She threatened to shoot the mare from under me.'

'Good morning, Polly,' Grat called, coming across the street to join them. 'This shifty character won't be bothering you no more. He's for the high jump. You'll be coming home with me. Ma's waiting for us. So we better get this over quick.'

'Yeah, mister,' Rigney snarled, propelling Matt back along the sidewalk. 'You're gonna kick air.'

There was nothing Matt could do. He was marched to a half-built cabin opposite the saloon.

'Enjoy your last few minutes on earth,' Rigney said.

Meanwhile Grat was rehearsing Poulson on the part he had to play, thrusting a hand-written page under his nose. 'You read this out, otherwise Harri slits your wife's throat. Got it?'

Grat grinned widely, beckoning to the men he had placed strategically on rooftops and in doorways to stay put. He frogmarched Poulson along to the makeshift gallows and, taking a stand, began ringing a handbell. Shutters and doors were opened and people peered out. 'Come an' jine us,' Grat shouted. 'We're gonna have a hanging.'

'I can't miss this,' Harriet yelled, yanking the two women along the sidewalk with her by the ropes around their necks. 'We're gonna git the best view.'

A small crowd of curious onlookers had gathered. Their faces registered surprise and shock to see Matthew Saunders in bonds. Grat jammed Poulson's bullet-holed top hat on to his head and announced, 'Mister Mayor will read the charges against the prisoner.'

In an unsteady voice Poulson stammered, 'The prisoner has been found guilty of complicity in the murder of Mr Joshua Vincent, guilty of cattle rustling, destruction of property, also the murder of several honest men in order to sustain his reign of terror.'

Poulson stumbled over the further names of so-called murdered men. 'Clive Mason, Abe Simpson and Seth Jones, visitors to this town, robbed of their cash, horses and possessions, murder of ramrodder of the Tarantula ranch, Dusty Stevens, and other Tarantula cowboys. . . .'

'These are all lies,' Matt shouted at the crowd. 'I didn't kill any of them apart from Abe and that was self-defence.'

Grat rang his handbell and nudged Poulson, who read from the sheet, 'Matthew Saunders has been tried and sentenced to death by hanging.'

'This man has deceived you all,' Grat shouted. 'He was plotting to take over my ranch and this town. His greed has undone him. The sentence will now be carried out.'

Luther White was propping a ladder up against a crossbeam of the building, tossing a hanging noose over the beam. He placed the noose over Saunders's head as he was brought before him. 'I'd better cut his wrist bonds,' he said, 'so he can climb up the damn ladder.'

'OK,' Grat nodded. 'Saunders, get up there and balance on that beam. Don't s'pose you've been strung up afore, but you'll soon get the hang of it.' He chuckled heartily. 'Get it?'

When Matt was sitting on the beam a dozen feet above the ground, looking decidedly unhappy, Grat called, 'You got any last words 'fore you jump!'

'You know this ain't right, Grat.'

'Matt speak true,' Katzenjammer shouted from his

barbershop doorway. 'He good man. You should not do this.'

'Not on a Sunday,' Mrs McGinty put in.

'Sunday, Monday, who gives a damn?' Grat roared, 'Jump into the pit of hell, you fiend.'

'No!' Polly screamed, trying to break away from Harriet. 'You're the murderer, Grat. You, your father, your mother, Harriet, are the cause of all this trouble.'

'Shut up,' Harriet snarled, slapping her. 'I'm sorry, Matt. If I cain't have you, nobody can.'

Luther had hitched the end of the rope tight to a support, which would allow for a three-foot drop. It probably wouldn't break his neck but he would die of strangulation after two or three minutes. 'Jump, you coward,' he roared.

There was nothing else for it. Matt took one last look at the blue sky, at Polly and launched himself off the beam, jerked to a halt, kicking and struggling, trying to hold on to the rope above him with his freed hands.

A hush fell over the crowd as they watched. Suddenly they gasped as a shot cracked out; the rope parted and Matt Saunders hit the ground hard.

The Longbranch cowboys came galloping along the street. Dave in the lead had aimed his carbine carefully and successfully at the rope. Earlier in the morning he had found a gold coin left by one of the Mexicans which had slipped down the side of his bunk, and had invited the men to celebrate in town. But it was not going to be a happy celebration.

As the cowboys hauled their mounts, in shooting irons blazing over the heads of the hanging crowd, Grat Vincent hurriedly returned fire, knocking one of the cowboys, Jim Heath, from the saddle and backing away into a doorway to save his skin.

Hired gun Ned Blair took aim from up behind the false front of the gun shop and another Longbranch boy, Randy Quaid, was sent spinning. Others of the Tarantula men showed themselves, sending a volley of lead at the cowboys, who wheeled their ponies and turned tail, seeking safer positions.

Jake Rigney had pulled his powerful six-gun from his shoulder holster, but Dave charged his horse, bowling him over, offering an arm to Matt, who scrambled to his feet and swung up behind him, and they galloped away down the street.

Meanwhile, Polly had kicked Harriet in the shins and jabbed her elbow into her abdomen, making her howl and double up. She wrenched the knife from the girl's hand, cut the ropes from her and Mrs Poulson's throats and they ran for safety. Harriet scrambled to her feet, pulling her twin shooters and sending shots carooming after them.

'Yeah, run, you chickens,' she howled. 'I'll ruffle your feathers later.'

She had to turn to defend herself for Katzenjammer was firing a rifle from his doorway, his bullet

sending her hat flying, and Eph Smith, the blacksmith, had hurled a hammer at Rigney, knocking
him over as he tried to regain his feet.

The crowd had scattered for safety, but many were
incensed at events. Even Wang Hu had come from
his laundry, aiming a little-used handgun at Blair, a
lucky shot somersaulting him from behind the false
front to land in a horse trough where he gurgled his
last.

As bullets flew from all directions, Luther White
backed away, firing, up the steps to the saloon. Gus
poked his shotgun from the window, blasted lead
into his back, which spun Luther off the sidewalk to
lie in the mud riddled with bloody holes.

Matt was groggily rubbing his throat as Dave and
what remained of his men dismounted. 'Keep calm,
men,' he croaked out. 'This ain't your fight. Give me
your gun, Dave, this is between me and Grat.'

The latter and Rigney had gained the safety of the
restaurant, taking potshots from the doorway at any
adversaries. Horace Poulson cowered behind them.
'You're finished, Grat. The whole town's against you,'
he ventured. 'Why don't you give up, avoid any more
bloodshed?'

'I ain't giving up,' Grat screamed, his face mania-
cal, his eyes bulging. 'I'll show 'em. I'll burn this
town to the ground.' He dashed out, making a
beeline for Coal Oil Charlie's kerosene store, reaching it and hurling himself inside.

'The guy's crazy,' Rigney muttered, licking his lips, nervously, as he checked his handgun. 'Is everybody crazy in this city?'

'Things are a trifle explosive,' Poulson agreed. 'If I were you I'd go back to Miles City as fast as you can.'

'No way, buster,' Rigney gritted out. 'We need to finish this.'

The cabin was stacked with cans of coal oil fuel. Grat shouldered Charlie out of the way, grabbed two of them and dashed out of the back door and along to the rear of the Washoe City saloon. He emptied the first can liberally against the tinder-dry cotton-wood boards, found a match, struck it and set the oil alight. He stood back as the flames spritzed streaking up the side of the saloon.

'How do they like that?' he screamed, and ran along the back of the barber shop where he did the same with the second can. Again the flames found instant purchase and, fanned by the prairie wind, started to creep up the wall of the next door restaurant. 'I'll burn you all down!'

Soon the saloon and several houses adjoining along that side of the street were a blazing inferno as startled men, screaming women and children ran from them.

Through the smoke and chaos Matt Saunders stepped resolutely and suddenly saw Grat standing on a corner laughing and jeering at the crowd, his revolver in his hand. Across the road from him Jake

156

Rigney had Poulson by the scruff of his neck as he edged towards the terrified horses at a hitching rail, looking for means of escape. He had decided to take the mayor's advice.

All three men saw each other at the same time. Matt was caught in their crossfire as they let loose lead at him. He stood firm as their bullets spat about him. He carefully aimed Dave's carbine at Grat, taking him out with his first shot. Grat scrambled to his knees, almost a pleading look on his face. Matt levered another slug into the breech and hit him with a heart shot, knocking him on to his back.

At the same time Rigney's bullet hit him in the shoulder, catapulting him off his feet and he rolled into the cover of the horse trough. Harriet came from the side alley of the burning saloon, her twin six-guns in her fist. 'Kill him,' she shouted. 'He don't deserve to live.'

But, as she loosed lead, the tall brick chimney collapsed and she screamed as it crashed down, pinning her beneath it. 'Aagh!' she groaned with her last breath.

Rigney hurled Poulson from him, running to grab one of the rearing mustangs and scrambled into the saddle, kicking its sides, galloping from the stricken town. But as he passed the livery Eph came running out with his rifle, fired and Jake Rigney rolled from the saddle across the dirt to lay still. Eph took a look and put another bullet in him to make sure.

Polly ran out to kneel beside Matt. 'Are you all right?'

'Well, I'm still alive.' He looked around grimly, amid the burning buildings and the bodies adorning the street. 'But I guess a lot ain't.'

Polly helped him to his feet. 'Where's Harriet?' he asked.

'There's nothing we can do for her. She's dead. Come on, Matt, I'm taking you home.' She found Crackers and helped him aboard, riding Poulson's mare herself. As they trotted away through the flames and carnage, Dave and the other cowboys, carrying their two dead, slung over mustangs, fell in behind them.

'Looks like we won,' Dozy Dave said.

An unexpected outcome of these events was that Martha died soon afterwards and the only kin, Polly, inherited the Tarantula ranch. So now she and Matt owned the whole length of Gun Barrel Valley.

Two months had passed since the inferno and slayings at Washoe City. Fire was not an unusual hazard in the West and the citizens had soon rebuilt the burned-out buildings. There was a new sense of camaraderie in the town.

Matt's shoulder wound had healed well, and although the stallion took a lot of strength to hold, he was back in the saddle and on this mid-summer morning galloping across the sage, gave the stallion his head and charged on, a glorious exhilaration of partnership between man and horse as they reached a crest of the high country.

Elk were bugling along in the breaks, an eagle spiralling up in the blue sky, sage hens warbling in the grass as he eased to a halt and looked back at Polly on Crackers toiling up to join him. 'Where did you get to?' he laughed.

Crackers had become a pal of the stallion, his presence calming him, and as Polly rested in the saddle in her new summer gingham dress and straw hat, she admired the view of the distant Rockies and breathed out, 'I've fallen in love with these vast spaces.'

'Not with *me*?' Matt quipped. 'Come on, I'll introduce you to a friend.'

Spotted Eagle seemed pleased to see them, his feathered braves gathering round to admire both the horse and the woman.

One, a slim, graceful warrior, Wolf Voice, almost naked but for a breech cloth, the Cheyenne's distinctive high collar, moccasins and a revolver in a beaded sheath hanging from his belt, took Polly's hand and stroked the palm in an enticing manner, mockery glimmering in his dark eyes as he stared at her. He raised a fist, opening and closing it four times.

'What is he saying?' Polly asked.

'He says he will give twenty ponies for you,' Matt told her, pulling her into him to indicate she was not for sale. 'Looks like I got competition. The sooner we git to Billings and find that preacher the better it'll be.'

'And the happier I'll be,' Polly smiled, kissing him. 'Oh dear, Wolf Voice made me feel quite strange.'

Spotted Eagle laughed, indicating two girls who wore their skirts short to display the self-inflicted scars of wounds flagellated on their shapely legs when they had lost their braves in battle, and made sign to say Wolf Voice already had three wives.

'Come eat in my tipi,' he signed. 'The days of hatred are gone.'

'Let's hope so,' the young rancher replied.

Polly gripped Matt's hand. 'I can hardly believe Uncle Joshua hated these people so bitterly.'

'Yeah,' Matt said. 'It's a strange world.'